*Look what people are saying about
this talented author...*

"Super-wonderful" and "smokin' hot."
—PAL "MORWA Books" on *Under His Spell*

"*Under His Spell* is a quirky story of romance and
circumstance. A fun, short read."
—*Fresh Fiction reviews*

"[A] pretty intense story at times with
the right amount of humor and tenderness
to balance it out."
—Review of *Under His Spell* by Queen B,
www.royallybitchy.blogspot.com

"Jade Lee wrote *The Dragon Earl* with gentle
humor and her signature passionate interludes. Her
engaging characters rapidly drew me in to their
dilemma, and I was tickled that I was enjoying this
lovely historical romance novel so much."
—*Publishers Weekly*

"I enjoyed the sensual and hot love scenes and
boy were they hot. WOW!"
—*Night Owl Romance* on *Dragonborn*

"A wonderfully strong-willed heroine engages
in a seductive battle of wits with a decidedly
unconventional hero in this refreshingly different,
sexy Regency romance."
—*Chicago Tribune* on *The Dragon Earl*

Blaze

Dear Reader,

One night, my fiancé had a huge project due at work that required a ton of data entry. Because I loved him, I agreed to help. We finally got it done at 2:00 a.m. when, flushed with elation, we realized that we were alone in a huge office building. And given that he worked in an electronics firm, my mind quickly danced through a zillion gadget and gizmo fantasies.

I will never tell what exactly happened that night, but suffice it to say that I had much more imagination than stamina. I will also confess that we did not resort to raiding the lab. Turns out there's a lot you can do in an office that has nothing to do with high-end electronics!

So there you have it. My deep, dark secret: I have office fantasies. Thankfully, I was able to put some of them to paper in *Taking Care of Business*. It helps that I modeled my hero after my own special geek of a husband, a man with more integrity than sense, more heart than hunkiness. Hopefully you'll fall in love with him as quickly as I did.

Sincerely,

Kathy Lyons

Kathy Lyons

TAKING CARE OF BUSINESS

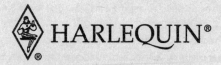

HARLEQUIN®

TORONTO • NEW YORK • LONDON
AMSTERDAM • PARIS • SYDNEY • HAMBURG
STOCKHOLM • ATHENS • TOKYO • MILAN • MADRID
PRAGUE • WARSAW • BUDAPEST • AUCKLAND

Recycling programs
for this product may
not exist in your area.

ISBN-13: 978-0-373-79580-2

TAKING CARE OF BUSINESS

Copyright © 2010 by Katherine Grill

This edition published by arrangement with Harlequin Books S.A.

For questions and comments about the quality of this book
please contact us at Customer_eCare@Harlequin.ca.

® and TM are trademarks of the publisher. Trademarks indicated with ® are registered in the United States Patent and Trademark Office, the Canadian Trade Marks Office and in other countries.

www.eHarlequin.com

Printed in U.S.A.

ABOUT THE AUTHOR

USA TODAY bestselling author Kathy Lyons loves writing light, funny, sexy stories for Harlequin Blaze and leaves the dark, tortured love stories to her alter ego, Jade Lee. In her spare time, Kathy loves kicking butt on a racquetball court. Jade, on the other hand, loves kicking back and watching the SyFy channel with her husband. Visit them both on the web at www.kathylyons.com or www.jadeleeauthor.com!

Books by Kathy Lyons

HARLEQUIN BLAZE

535—UNDER HIS SPELL

1

THANK GOD FOR COFFEE, James Samuel Finn thought as he reached for his triple venti latte.

"I made it extra sweet," said the barista with a smile. "You look like you could use it this morning."

Sam gave her a rueful smile as he dropped a generous tip in the jar. "At least I got the project done."

"Good for you," she quipped as she turned to the next customer.

Yes, Sam thought as he took that first glorious sip. Good for him, but more importantly, good for his company. He'd stayed up all night putting together the prototype, hence the celebratory latte. He just had time to polish up the presentation, change out of his lab coveralls, and make it to the board meeting at ten. And didn't he just feel like the genius inventor that everyone thought he was.

"Get out of the way, you old bat!" bellowed a cabbie. "You're blocking the road!"

Sam started, looking up from his drink and blinking rapidly against the bright sunlight. It wasn't hard to find the source of the problem. An older woman, probably in her seventies, was trying to parallel park an old Crown Victoria. The thing was too big for downtown Chicago parking spaces, and the woman was too short to see well over the dash as she inched her way into the spot. Meanwhile, traffic was backing up behind her, led by one extremely irate cab driver.

"Come on, lady. You shouldn't be driving, and you know it!"

"That's enough!" Sam snapped as he stepped forward. The woman needed help, not insults. He stepped out into traffic, completely blocking the cab who was now trying to squeeze his car around hers. The bastard started cursing up a blue streak, but Sam ignored him. Instead, he gestured for the woman to roll down her window.

She did, and he gently began directing her into the parking spot. It wasn't that hard. Once she had someone else's eyes to rely on, she relaxed and the car slid easily into place.

"Oh, thank you!" she breathed gratefully. "The parking garage was full, and I didn't know what else to do! I never come out into the city, but my grandson fell and broke his teeth, and this was the only time the dentist had available. Usually my daughter…"

She rambled on, obviously still upset. Meanwhile, the cabbie finally streaked past, throwing more insults as he left.

"Don't worry about it," Sam said as he waved to the eight-year-old in the back seat. "Those guys give Chicago a bad name."

"No, no," the woman said as she finally killed the engine. "He's right. I should get a smaller car, but we can't afford it. And this old monstrosity has been with me for twenty years."

Sam's tired brain kicked into gear as she got her grandson out of the car and headed toward the dentist. She was a perfect candidate for his prototype. He'd designed a strip of sensors that attached to anything—robot, wheelchair, massively old car—and gave a beautiful display that anyone could read. There was even a state-of-the-art verbal interface. Making a sudden decision, Sam popped open his cell phone and called Roger, his best friend and CFO.

An hour later, the grandson's teeth were done, Sam's coveralls were streaked with street grime and engine grease, and the Crown Victoria had his brand-new prototype attached to its body. He'd even rigged a dashboard attachment for the display.

"See," he explained to Mrs. Evans. "You won't have any problems maneuvering out of the parking spot now. You can see right on the display exactly how far you can move."

"Why, it's just like on those fancy new cars!"

Sam nodded. The system was actually a great deal more powerful than what was in new-model vehicles, but that wasn't important to Mrs. Evans. All she cared about was that she'd be able to park with confidence now, even in her huge Crown Vic.

"We'll be in contact in a few weeks to find out how it's working out for you," he said as she started up her car. Then he stepped back and watched her maneuver out of her parking spot like a champ. She was halfway down the street when Roger finally spoke up.

"You realize that equipment is worth far more than her car."

"We need real-world testing," he answered as he took a sip of his latte. Damn, it had gone cold. He'd been so hurried trying to get the prototype installed before

Kevin's teeth were done that he hadn't drunk his latte. Now it was ice cold.

"Yes," Roger concurred, "but we need to test it in harsh environments like a NASA test center or a deep ocean oil rig."

"Chicago city streets *are* a harsh environment," Sam shot back.

"Yeah? And what are you going to show to the board in..." Roger glanced at his watch. "In less than an hour?"

Sam grimaced as he threw away his latte and headed into the office building, Roger trailing behind. "I don't know," he said. "I'll think of something."

"This isn't the time to be taking big risks, you know. Did you look at the last spreadsheets I sent you? Not just opened the email, but actually read it?"

Sam nodded absently as they entered the building. Usually, he'd go to the back service elevator, especially since his coveralls were covered in grime. But a vision in yellow swept past him, and Sam's libido took control. Instead of turning left, he swung right to follow the woman. Or maybe he was just trying to ditch Roger.

Unfortunately, his right-hand man was not so easily distracted. "I've put together a slick package to distract the board," he was saying, "but they certainly have read the spreadsheets, even if you haven't. Please tell me—"

"Who's that woman?" Sam asked, tilting his head toward the vision in a flowing yellow sundress. It wasn't just the dress that made her stand out. It was her smile and the way she walked—all confidence and positive outlook. Given that she was surrounded by dark suited office stiffs, she stood out like the sun on a dreary day.

"What?" Roger frowned at his friend. "Aren't you dating Cindy?"

Sam shook his head. "Broke up six…er, seven months ago."

"Really? Why?"

Sam shrugged. The same reason he'd stopped seeing Marty and Josie and Tammy. "She wanted James S. Finn, multimillionaire, not plain old Sam."

Roger snorted. "That's because Sam dresses in coveralls and smells like engine grease."

Sam didn't answer. He was too busy maneuvering so that he could get into the same elevator as the woman in yellow.

JULIE THOMPSON WAS DRESSED for battle. Not in armor or anything, but in a bright yellow sundress and sandals that made her feel sexy, beautiful and beyond brilliant. In this outfit, nothing could stop her. Not an ad campaign that refused to come together. Not rent coming due on both her minuscule apartment and her office space on the seventeenth floor. And certainly not poor Harry, a young lawyer on her floor, who was buried under three huge boxes of folders.

"Goodness, Harry, doesn't the law firm have a dolly for stuff like this?"

Harry gave her a sad laugh. "Why have that when you can force the first-years to lug the crap?"

They were standing in the elevator alcove, waiting their turn. She could tell by the bags under his eyes that the guy hadn't gotten much sleep. And if his rumpled suit was anything to judge by, what little rest he'd gotten had been in these clothes.

"Come on. How heavy can it be?" she asked as she reached forward and lifted off the top box. "Umph!"

Heavy didn't even cover it. Apparently, the law firm made the first-years lug files weighted with lead.

"Don't do that—" cried Harry, but Julie was already shaking her head.

"I've carried much heavier stuff. Trust me."

He gave her a grateful smile as the elevator dinged. "You're the best." Then they both waited as the people in front of them maneuvered into the cramped lift.

As this was a huge downtown high-rise, that was a ton of people. Amid the suited professionals from one firm or another, she also caught sight of one of the bigwigs from the robotics firm on the top floor. He was standing next to a janitor or something. The guy wore dirty coveralls and had a dead leaf caught in his hair. Whatever he'd just been doing, it hadn't been easy. Still, he looked cute even with the grease stain across his forehead. And with his sleeves rolled up like that, she could see his muscular forearms. It was silly to notice a guy's forearms, but she did. And she liked the way he smiled at her.

"Excuse me, excuse me," murmured Harry as he pushed his way into the elevator.

"Maybe we should wait," Julie suggested. There really wasn't room for everyone plus the boxes.

Harry flashed her a look of apology. "I'm kinda late. Let me just take the box—"

"No, no," Julie returned. "You've already got the other two. We'll all fit," she said hopefully.

It was hard maneuvering herself and the huge box of files in. She turned around to face the front, apologizing to an accountant from the fifth floor as she jostled him. Harry had managed to somehow push their floor button, so Julie tried to back up enough to allow the doors to close.

It was a tight fit. It was a really, really tight fit, and she ended up backing into the guy in coveralls. She knew because she could feel the heavy cotton against her backside. Then the accountant elbowed her, shoving her even farther back. She stumbled. Not badly. Hell, both of her legs could be broken and she would be still standing upright in this cramped space. But it did force her bottom to bump hard against...

Oh my! That wasn't a zipper she felt pressed hot and hard against her rear. That was coveralls-guy getting a very human reaction to her pressed against him. She ought to feel mortified. She ought to feel embarrassed for them both. Especially since there was nothing either of them could do, crammed together the way they were. All she could do was stand there pressed against his erection.

What to do? What to do? She didn't know, but for the first time in months, she stopped thinking about her company slowly going belly-up. She stopped worrying about how she would pay her next bill or drum up her next contract. Her entire mind was absorbed with feeling a strange man against her backside. A *well-endowed* strange man.

And in that moment, a bizarre sense of daring hit her. After all, no one could see what was happening. They were shoved into the back corner, completely anonymous and yet completely intimate. Without her even planning it, biology took over. She allowed herself to drop a little farther back onto Mr. Coverall, and then she squeezed. Yup. Right there. She squeezed him for all she was worth.

She heard his gasp of shock and had to work to cover her smile. Good lord, had she just molested a perfect stranger? Apparently so because as the doors pulled open, she felt an answering pressure from him. Was he thrusting against her? Oh. My. God! She was both excited and appalled by the situation. And turned on like she hadn't been in months.

And then, damn it, the ride was over. They had arrived at the seventeenth floor. Julie stepped forward because she had to. She didn't even dare look behind her to see his face. Was his as red as hers? Was what they'd just done written on the blush that she knew was staining her cheeks?

She followed Harry to the law office, handed off the box to another first-year, and then headed to her own suite. Web Wit and Wonder was her very own advertising firm, started with best friend and brilliant graphic artist, Karen Wilson. Unfortunately, it was going under. That was why she'd worn this dress today. So she could bolster her confidence as she tackled one last bid for a contract. Except now, all she could think about was Elevator Man and how she'd...

"Good morning!" called Karen as Julie entered their office suite. "I brought muffins..." Her voice trailed away as she looked at her friend. "And my, don't you look flushed today."

Hell. There was no fooling Karen's eagle eye. "Um. Yeah. I think I need some coffee." Julie set down her purse and went straight for the cappuccino machine. Everything else in their office was stripped down to the bare essentials. But this lovely thing was an office-warming present from her parents. Sadly, that hadn't been all they'd given her. They'd also loaned her money to start the business. And if Web Wit and Wonder didn't get a new contract soon, that debt was going to go unpaid.

"Come on, Julie. What happened?"

Julie sighed. She knew she'd never get to work if she didn't tell her friend the truth. "It's no big deal," she said. "Just, well, something happened in the elevator."

She told Karen it all. Everything in glorious detail so she could relive the thrill of it. She'd never been someone to go for anonymous sex, much less today's weird elevator fondle, but there was something so thrilling in what she'd done. As if she were suddenly scandalous or incredibly daring. It had just been a butt squeeze in a full elevator, but right then, she felt like she'd walked on the dark side. And Karen, bless her, found it just as exciting.

"You have to do it again!" Karen pressed.

"No!" Julie countered. "Besides, how could I?"

"Don't be ridiculous. I get crammed into elevators all the time. You just have to keep an eye out for your guy and make sure to—"

"What I'm going to do is focus on this campaign. Our proposal has to be perfect."

Karen paused a moment, then huffed in disgust. "Fine, fine. All work and no play makes you a dull girl."

Julie bit her lip, wondering just how much of the dollar and cents her artistic partner understood about their company. "Um, you know, I was going over our books last night and the picture—"

"I know," Karen interrupted, holding up her hand to silence her friend. "Well, I don't know the exact figures, but I've got a pretty good idea."

Julie nodded. There was nothing more to say to that. Except, perhaps, that they would get through this.

"We're going to put together a kick-ass proposal. We're going to be brilliant."

"And we're going to win this contract," Karen echoed with confidence. "I just know it."

2

Seven weeks later...

"WE DIDN'T GET THE contract." Julie stared at her laptop, her mind going numb. "We didn't get it."

Across the desk, Karen sighed and set down her sketchbook. Neither one of them had to say what they were thinking. They were both far from home, buried in debt, and as of five minutes ago, their company was dead. Bankrupt. Belly-up. *Finito.*

"This should have worked," Julie said as she fell back in her chair and stared at the ceiling tiles. "I think and breathe advertising. You're the best graphic designer there is. And together we know the internet like the back of our hands. We should be buried in accounts, not..." Dead broke.

Karen released another heavy sigh. "Yeah, okay, so this campaign didn't work. It was brilliant, they're idiots for not hiring us, but now we have to move on. So, what's next?"

Julie didn't answer. She didn't have the heart to tell her best friend that after two years of scrimping and sweating and bleeding, she just didn't have it in her to try again. She'd put everything into this last pitch: heart, soul, and her last borrowed dime. They'd failed anyway. They hadn't gotten the account.

"My dad's started a new bowling league," she said, still talking to the ceiling tiles.

"In Nebraska?" Karen snorted. "You hate Nebraska!"

She hated starving, too. And being homeless. Which she would soon be since she couldn't pay any more rent on her tiny apartment or on this cramped office space.

"Come on, Julie. Usually you're the one with six more possibilities lined up, just in case. So what's next? What have you got up your sleeve?"

"Nothing," she whispered. "Absolutely nothing. We're done."

Karen was silent for a long time, clearly absorbing the finality of that while Julie tried hard to *not* think of returning to Nebraska, suitcase in hand. How did she tell her family that her plan to make it big—the one she'd talked about since she was twelve years old—had ended up in a huge pile of debt?

"Okay, I've got a new plan," Karen said firmly. "I think you should get laid."

Julie lifted her head to stare at her friend. "What?"

"I'm serious. You've been working nonstop for months. Years, even. Too much tension stops the flow of qi."

"What?"

"Your energy, your power. And nothing else opens up the qi like a good—"

"Karen! You can't possibly think that sex is an answer to bankruptcy." There. She'd said the word aloud.

Her friend shook her head. "We're not closed yet. We've got almost a month left for you to think of something brilliant. But you won't think of anything with your qi all clogged."

Julie didn't answer. Her friend was being silly as a way to lighten the mood. It was sweet really, but some things couldn't be changed regardless of her state of qi.

Karen leaned forward, dropping her elbows onto Julie's desk. "When was the last time you saw Elevator Man?"

Julie nearly choked. Gawd, she should never have told her friend about *him*. Especially since the elevator seven weeks ago had only been the first incident. They'd had approximately one anonymous encounter a week since then. And that was nothing compared to her nighttime fantasies. Who'd have thought that she would become obsessed with elevator sex? But she had. She didn't know whether her fantasies were fueling her forays into the scandalous or the reverse, but whatever the reason, she'd been unable to stop herself from orchestrating increasingly sexual encounters with the hunky janitor.

Their second time had been in another jam-packed elevator, but this time she'd gotten in first. She hadn't even been sure it was him except that his general height and build were the same. He was about six foot and lean in those blue denim coveralls. His hair was rich brown, all curly and shaggy, and his shoulders broad. As she'd stared at his dark, dark brown eyes, she'd wondered: *are you him? Are you the first man to touch me in forever?*

He hadn't answered, of course. But he'd inhaled deeply, and she'd thought about her perfume. Was he smelling the sandalwood she liked to dab on her wrists? Or the minty herb of her shampoo? Did he know what she was thinking?

She'd smiled at him, then. Something in her had taken over and she'd flashed her best come-hither smile. He'd seen it. His gaze zeroed in on her lips. But he didn't do anything, didn't say anything. If anything, his eyes had gone impersonal and vague.

Her ego had crashed. This wasn't her elevator man. Or if it was, he wasn't interested in her. She had been stunned by the pain of that. The disappointment had cut deep, probably because she'd built so many erotic daydreams about him. She'd just been biting back a sigh when he reached forward to press the button for his floor.

Top floor. No biggie. Except on his way to the panel, he'd brushed across her right breast. It could have been an accident. After all, there were a dozen people crammed into the elevator. There was hardly space to breathe, much less reach for a button. But he *had* brushed her breast and her nipple reacted with a nearly painful point.

And on the way back from pressing the button, he'd done it again. Or perhaps she had "accidentally" pushed forward so that he had no choice but to caress her hard nipple. That was it for Encounter 2.

Encounter 3 came the next week, this time on the way down to the garage. Half-packed elevator, close quarters, but she'd been wearing a suit jacket so there was no accidental nipple brushing. But Elevator Man was nothing if not innovative.

He'd murmured, "Excuse me, excuse me," as he maneuvered to stand right in front of her. Then he knelt down to open an access panel beneath the floor buttons.

Everyone had shifted to accommodate him. Everyone, that is, except her because his position on the floor left his elbow pressed to her mons.

Oh, God, it had felt so good. Pressure. A circular rub. The garage floor had come too soon, and she'd been too chicken to stay. That night's fantasy, however, had involved an empty elevator stuck between floors. It was only after encounters five and six that she migrated to a glass one at the top of the Eiffel Tower. She was pressed up against the glass while he did her hot and hard in front of the whole of Paris.

Yes, she was depraved, but perhaps that was the thrill of it. He was always polite, always gentle, and he stopped the moment the elevator did. But he made her feel like she was the hottest woman on the planet, like he couldn't stop himself from touching her. She knew the shape of his body, the scent of his hair and the feel of his cock through a thousand encounters both real and imagined. And she couldn't wait until it happened again.

And now, here was Karen asking for the details. "This last one was, um, the best," she said, her face heating to crimson. "He stepped up behind me, pulled my hips back against his, and then…"

"Yes? What?"

Julie bit her lip. "His hand slid forward to, um, cup me. God, he has the best hands—big and strong."

"Oh, my God! What did you do?"

Julie closed her eyes, unable to look at her friend in the face as she confessed this. "Nothing," she whispered. "I just, well, enjoyed it." But she'd thought about more. She'd thought about spreading her legs and giving in. She wanted to. She'd wanted to for weeks now, but she was too chicken. What if he told someone? What if he told a client? Of course, that wasn't a problem now. There were no more clients—potential or otherwise. Meanwhile, she could still feel the imprint of his hand on her. God, it made her twist in hunger just thinking about it. It was a wonder she didn't combust right here.

"Soo," drawled Karen with a knowing look. "Sounds like you should enjoy things some more. Just do it, Julie. Let yourself go for once in your life. It'll reset your qi."

"Stop! I can't just do someone in the elevator."

"Of course you can. You got condoms?"

Julie nodded. She'd bought them weeks ago, and they'd been burning a hole in her purse ever since. She wanted to use them. It was insane, but she'd been thinking about it for two months now. She wanted to stop the elevator, hand him the condom and let herself do what she'd been fantasizing about.

"Meanwhile," Karen said with a heavy sigh. "I've got to get home. Tomorrow's lecture awaits." Thankfully, Karen also taught at the Chicago School of Design. The collapse of their company would require a box of Kleenex and another of chocolates, but she wouldn't be out on the street. Julie, on the other hand, would have to sell her laptop to pay for the bus ride home.

"Hey!" Karen cried as she playfully swiped at Julie's leg with her portfolio. "Don't stay here all night stewing. Go find Elevator Man. Or someone else."

"Karen—"

"Seriously. Something will come up. Just have faith."

Would it? Julie wondered. And if it did, did she still have the heart to pursue it? Instead of answering, she gave her friend a warm smile. "You're the best," she said. "I'm glad I picked you to go belly-up with."

"Three more weeks," Karen returned. "We're not done until the rent expires in three weeks." Then she was gone, heading out into the darkened expanse of the downtown office building.

Julie didn't speak as their suite door clicked shut. She couldn't. Her throat had clogged up and her eyes were watering. Three weeks or three years, it didn't matter. She just didn't think she had the heart to keep trying. Besides, she told herself sternly, she wanted to go home. She missed her family. What she couldn't get past was that she'd be returning home a failure. A bankrupt failure.

It was on her twelfth birthday that she'd started talking about making it big in the big city. Her two younger brothers had laughed. Her sister, too, right after she'd said, "Julie always tells stories." Even her mom had patted her head as if to say, isn't she cute, dreaming the impossible dream. Only her father had taken her side. He'd told her then she could do anything she wanted, even move to Chicago and make her fortune.

It had taken fifteen years to make her dream a reality—or so she'd thought. But now she realized that her sister was right. Web Wit and Wonder was just another story that never came true. Pushing away that morose thought, she turned to her laptop and started typing. She stayed at her desk for hours more, searching for something, anything, to tide them over for another month. She didn't find it. No jobs for an ad agency. Nothing even for a talented copywriter. She was out of options and out of money. It was time to go home.

Glancing at her clock, she was startled to see that it was nearly ten. Way too late for Elevator Man. She would have to count on her own fantasies for relief tonight. Just as well. She was feeling much too vulnerable right then. She didn't even have a plant to go home to. Nothing but the ever-present certainty that she'd failed.

She closed up her laptop with a definitive click. She didn't have a coat today despite the early fall cold snap. She'd chosen instead a wrap sweater top over dress pants. It was soft and warm, a gift from her younger sister for her birthday. Wearing it felt like being wrapped in cashmere love, though it was simple cotton. And except for Elevator Man, it was the only thing that had caressed her in a very long time. She must have known this morning that she'd need a hug by night.

Her thoughts were getting too morose. "Tomorrow, I can begin again," she said out loud as a way to bolster her spirits. She stepped into the dark corridor, locking the office door behind her. The building was designed like a big rectangle around a central courtyard complete with trees and a water fountain. Way up high, the glass-paneled roof let in sunlight by day. Tonight, a big brilliant moon pierced the darkness. Only the robotics firm on the top floor had lights on. Robotics, apparently, weren't affected by the sluggish economy, unlike small advertising firms.

She walked to the elevator bank and pressed a button. Her thoughts returned to Elevator Man, and she sternly reminded herself not to hope. At this hour, he had surely gone home already. That left her free to imagine all sorts of wildly erotic scenarios. The elevator took a long time coming, so she was able to fully steep herself in her fantasies. She pictured him behind her and all of Paris spread out before them. She imagined the thrust of his erection, the caress of his hands on her body. She was a wild woman, desired by a hot guy and completely free to enjoy her body. No work, no cares, just a man taking her to the ultimate sexual peak. God, it was heaven!

She was smiling as the metal doors parted, then she gasped in surprise. There, leaning back against the glass rear panel was Elevator Man. His usual coveralls were gone. Instead, he wore sneakers, dark jeans and a well worn cotton tee. The color was indigo fading to gray. Whatever image had once been there was now long gone, leaving little to distract her from the rippled shadows created by his sculpted torso. God, his forearms were nothing compared to the muscles across his chest.

Lifting her gaze a little higher, she saw his chiseled jaw, slightly darkened by five o'clock shadow. His eyes were at half mast as his nostrils flared. He was inhaling, his chest expanding as he clearly took in the scent of her. She'd started dabbing heavy amounts of sandalwood on her wrists ever since she'd noticed he took a deep breath whenever he was near her.

She didn't speak. She couldn't. He was lounging against the back panel watching her with a predatory expression. As if he'd been waiting for her. As if he'd known she was getting on the elevator right then and was daring her to step into his lair.

Karen's words echoed in her mind. *Just do it. Let yourself go for once in your life.* Julie bit her lip. Could she? She had three weeks before she left Chicago for good. In three weeks, she would return to rural Nebraska and a wholly different life. Suddenly, three weeks felt like the perfect amount of time. Just enough time to revel in all her fantasies of the urban jungle. Three weeks to indulge however she wanted—passionately, frivolously, sexually—whatever she desired. Three weeks of time to be the wild woman she always pretended she was. After that, she would go home and start again.

All she had to do to begin was step through the door and let Elevator Man do whatever he wanted. Hell, she didn't even need to wait for him. She could stop the elevator herself and let him know she was willing. That she'd wanted this for the last two months. Could she do it?

Yes. Tonight she was going to reset her qi because why the hell not? Tonight, she was going to do what she'd been fantasizing about for months.

With that thought in mind, she crossed the threshold. Then she did what she always did at the beginning of one of their encounters. She turned around to face the elevator doors, though her back prickled with awareness of him right behind her. She extended her hand and pushed the garage floor button.

The elevator hummed to life, the doors shutting slowly. But Julie didn't let her hand drop away from the panel. Instead, her fingers hovered over the Stop button. *Now,* she told herself. *Pull the Stop button now!*

3

SAM FINN'S HEART—and dick—leaped forward, but he didn't move off the elevator wall. He feared if he shifted at all, nothing would stop him from grabbing Miss Julie Thompson and dragging her back to his cave, so to speak. So he held himself still and gripped the railing until his hands hurt.

She had paused before strutting into the elevator, her pert chin lifted in challenge and her hips swaying slightly in anticipation. Was tonight the night? Finally? After months of foreplay, would he finally get up the nerve to push them to the next level?

Nearly two months ago, Sam had also stood at the back of an elevator while *she* sauntered in. Later, he learned what her name was. Later, he figured out that she was the owner and creative force behind Web Wit and Wonder. Later, he realized that she'd been in her "creative" mode, dressing and walking with a flair that he found especially sexy.

At the time, all he noticed was that she was a bright flash of yellow sundress, bouncy hair and strappy sandal attitude. All woman, very perky in all the best ways, and a night-and-day difference from the corporate stiffs he was about to face in his own boardroom. Then she had stuffed her delectable body close, he'd caught the exotic scent of sandalwood, and his dick had the normal, predictable reaction. He'd gotten a boner the size of the Sears Tower.

Nothing unusual there. Every male above the age of eleven had suffered through an embarrassing erection. But then she'd done the unthinkable. She'd pressed backward against him. Far from being shocked and repelled, she'd actually, swear to God, squeezed him. Well, that's what his lower half believed. And then, while his brain was scrambling desperately to hold on to sanity, she had stepped away. Seconds later, she was off the elevator while he was harder than granite. He'd needed twenty minutes before he could face his employees.

It could have been an isolated incident, the kind of random thing that sometimes happened in a city the size of Chicago. It probably would have remained an isolated event if he weren't owner of the office building in which they both worked.

But he did own the building and he had access to all sorts of interesting security devices. Nothing intrusive, but it took less than a minute to learn everything official about Miss Thompson and her ad agency. And given that this was a building outfitted with the latest and greatest technology of the time, he could easily tie its security feed to his own laptop. There was no surveillance within her office suite. That would be a breach of privacy. But in the hallway outside her door? Absolutely. He knew when she came and went from her office, he knew what she wore, and most importantly, when she would be heading for the elevator banks.

So the stalking began. He couldn't get her out of

his mind. Had her caress been a product of his fevered imagination? Or would she welcome more? Could such a beautiful woman really want his touch? He had to know if he was imagining her response or if she was just into kinky, anonymous sex play.

It took nearly a week, but he'd managed to arrange to be in another packed elevator with her. His heart had been beating triple time, but after a week of fruitless speculation, he'd had to put the question to the test. He'd reached for the elevator button by way of her breast.

He'd tried to be subtle. If she started screaming, he could pretend he'd stumbled, it was an accident... He had an entire litany of excuses ready. He'd extended his hand, brushed across her breast and then pushed the button. And damn if on the way back, she didn't "accidentally" fall forward enough that he was nearly cupping her.

He'd almost collapsed. He had nearly convinced himself that she would scream bloody murder. That he'd be facing a sexual harassment lawsuit. But when none of that happened, his mind had simply shut down with shock. That, unfortunately, gave free rein to his inner stalker.

He'd never gone for emotionless sex before. Never had an interest in casual hook-ups. His life was his robotics company, and his women had been relationships. He never guessed that he would spend two months trying to find a way to have sex with a stranger in an elevator.

But maybe that was the point. Maybe he was ready for sex without pretense. Forget a meeting of minds and life goals. Julie Thompson was a bright splash of color in his very gray, very robotic world. Why couldn't he walk on the wild side for a while? As long as she was willing, he was game.

And best of all, he made sure he only connected with her when he was in his coveralls. He'd be damned if he let another woman have "sex with the billionaire." He hadn't thought there were that many money-hungry groupies in the world. Certainly not those who would go for a boring, nearsighted, robotics geek. But experience had taught him to be extra cautious about his identity. So, if Miss Julie Thompson wanted hot elevator sex, she was going to get it with a maintenance guy, not a CEO.

So the stalking began in earnest. He watched when she came and left her work. It helped that she was as much a workaholic as he was. Their hours matched up nicely. Morning elevator mash-ups allowed for discreet fondling. And at night, when he was all alone in his bed, he played out scenarios that appalled his rational brain.

But that was fantasy, and he was beyond tired of playing by himself. Tonight, she was here alone and he was more than ready to take it to the next level.

She had turned her back on him with a sexy wiggle to her hips. The scent of sandalwood hit him and his blood went straight south. If he were sticking to his usual pattern, this was when he would come up behind her and begin fondling. Her ass, her hips, her breasts—didn't matter. She was fantastic all around. Curvy, athletic without being obsessive, and just the right height for him, especially when she wore heels.

But this wasn't going to be a usual elevator encounter. It was late at night, they were the last ones in the building, and he had control of the elevator thanks to a new app he'd just installed on his phone.

The elevator started moving and he could see her body change. Her purse slid down her shoulder to land by her feet on the floor. Her shoulders opened up and her chin lifted slightly. And best of all, her hand hovered over the Stop button. Right there was the invitation he needed. She wanted more, just like he did. Was she going to do it? Was she going to pull the button?

Yes! She popped it out and a split second later, he initiated the app on his phone. Right on cue, the elevator jerked to a stop between floors, its security camera turning off at the same time. She gasped and stumbled, clearly surprised by the lurch. He caught her before she fell backward. His thighs braced her legs, and his arms went around her body, one over her right shoulder, the other curving around her lower ribs. She wore a soft sweater top that tied on one side. If he slid his hand across her belly, he could have her top undone with a flick of his wrist.

"Are you all right?" he said, his voice low.

"Y-yes," she stammered, turning her head. They were nearly nose to nose. He could smell the herbal scent to her hair and even his bad eyes could see the dark rich black of her eyelashes. "I, um, must have missed and hit the wrong button."

"Nah. We've been working on the elevators," he lied. "It's been acting wonky all day."

"Oh," she said softly, as she lifted her face to his. "That's too bad."

Now was the time, he told himself, and without thinking twice, he simply went for it.

SHE'D DONE IT. She'd stopped the elevator and now she had to follow through. She was trembling, her belly shivering where his hand held her so solidly. And his eyes were the most wonderful color of brown. A rich, dark chocolate that tempted her to dive right in and lap up all the goodness that he alone could give her.

His mouth touched hers, all warm and seductive. He brushed his lips across hers, teased her with his tongue.

"We're in no danger," he said, his voice a deep shiver across her skin. "I think I can start it up again," he continued. And while his mouth continued to tease hers, his hand skated over her belly and tugged at the tie of her top.

She gasped. Her lips felt incredibly sensitive, but nothing could top the knowledge that he was starting to undress her. Was she really going to do this? His kiss deepened, his tongue thrusting into her mouth as she opened to him. And she felt the tie of her sweater pull loose.

She broke the kiss. Not because she wanted it to end, but because she needed air.

He pulled back enough to look into her eyes. She saw his question clear as day. Would she allow him to take it further? Did she want this? Karen's "just go for it" words echoed in her mind.

Rather than answer, she stayed with the nonsensical chitchat. "I was working late. Big contract just fell through," she said. Then she gasped as his hand worked between the loose folds of her top to touch her bare skin. His fingers were calloused, the texture as erotic as his slow slide across her belly.

"I'm sorry," he murmured.

"So am I." She was still half reclined in his arms, and the position was a bit awkward. So she straightened, and he supported her, taking the opportunity to slide his other hand down from her shoulder to slip underneath the back of her top.

"I could call someone, if you like," he said, his voice a heated brush against her ear. He was giving her the opportunity to say no, to end things right now. But she didn't, firmly shaking her head.

"There's no need to bother anyone else."

As she moved, his hand on her belly flowed with her, rubbing across her abdomen, making her muscles tremble. And all the while, his other hand continued to whisper up her back to the clasp of her bra. She closed her eyes, her body tightening and her breath shallow.

"I'll fix the elevator as soon as you want," he said as he thumbed the catch on her bra. That was his way of telling her they could stop at any time.

"Not yet," she whispered, stunned by her own audacity. She had just said it. She had just told him that she wanted more from him. And sure enough, he took the invitation, moving both hands around her until he cupped her breasts.

God, yes! His hands were so large, he easily surrounded her, and his callouses provided just the right friction as they slid across her skin. She felt her back arch and her head drop back. His body pressed up against her, his heat warming her back. She leaned into him, letting her head fall onto his shoulder. She wanted to touch him, to feel his muscular strength. Her hands were down by her sides, so she reached behind her to stroke his thighs. God, he felt good. His thighs were corded, powerful with almost no give.

"I'm Sam," he said, his mouth against her ear.

Finally, she knew his name. "Julie," she gasped, and the movement thrust her breasts deeper into his palms. He was kneading her flesh, rolling her nipples slowly between his fingers. She moaned softly, the sound rumbling through her body into his. He brushed his jaw across her temple.

"I love the way you smell," he murmured. Then he shifted and nipped the curve of her ear. She shivered at the touch, surprised by the intensity of her reaction. Sex had never felt this way before, never this thrilling. Even more surprising was the way she reacted when he began to explore. It was as if her body had a whole new set of responses to his touch, and she was learning them at the same time he was.

When he squeezed her breasts, her breath eased and her skin heated. When he rolled her nipples, she moaned low and deep. But when he pinched them, especially when he accompanied that with a nip on her ear, she gasped and thrust backward against him. She didn't control her reactions, didn't know what was coming next. She just let herself feel while her body's hunger grew and grew.

"You are so hot," he said against her ear. She whimpered in response. One of his hands left her breast to brush down her belly. He paused with his fingers on the catch of her dress pants. "One look, and I can't think of anything but this. You've been driving me insane for two months."

Her breath shuttered to a stop, her mind making a desperate bid for sanity. He was going to open her pants, he was going to slide his fingers… Before she could finish the thought, he popped the button on her pants and slid down the zipper. She felt the rrrrr of the metal teeth as her trousers fell open and his fingers slid down over her thin panties.

She was so hot there and wet. And she couldn't think beyond the pressure of his fingers and the desire to finally feel him inside her. This was just like her fantasies. Better even, because the heat between them was so much larger, so much more powerful than even she had dreamed.

Then he did it. He slid over her mons and thrust his finger between her folds. A second later he was pushing ever so slowly inside her. She felt surrounded by him, held in place and caressed in the most intimate ways.

He was supporting most of her weight as her body arched into his caress. He thrust deep, impaling her with precision, before slowly pulling out, the length of his finger rolling over her clit. Her legs trembled and weakened. She had nothing to hold on to. Her hands kept sliding over his thighs, but he was too large for her to grip with any strength. She felt suspended in pleasure, adrift in sensation as he pinched her nipple while thrusting back inside her.

Her muscles gripped him, and her breath came in short gasps. Her body shuddered, her mind too splintered from the sensations to do more than experience. He was toying with her nipple, lengthening, squeezing, even twisting. While below, his tempo began to increase.

Her belly began to tighten, and her heart was pounding in her ears. "Oh! Oh!" She was keening softly, her word more like a high gasp. He played her masterfully, bringing her to the edge then holding her off. God, she was so close! Just a little more, a little more, and yet she wanted it to last forever. And then she couldn't stop. He thrust into her again and she met him, arching into his hand. And…

Yes!

4

JULIE FLOATED BACK FROM BLISS with a reluctant sigh. Which was rapidly followed by a burning flush of embarrassment. Was she really still standing? And had she really just let Elevator Man—Sam—finger her to orgasm?

His breathing was deep and even against her back. He was supporting her still, one hand on her hip, the other arm wrapped gently around her. God, he was so solid! She got the impression he could hold her like this all night if need be.

"Wow..." she began, unsure what to say. "What a great end to a sucky day."

She felt his chuckle rumble through her spine. "Building maintenance is a service-oriented field."

She laughed, really laughed at that. But there was only so much humor she could cling to before she became excruciatingly aware of her position. Shifting awkwardly, she reached down and pulled up her pants. He let her go, stepping back to a polite distance. She felt her face heat. Was there a polite distance after what they'd just done?

He cleared his throat awkwardly. "It, um, doesn't have to end right now. We could go out for a drink. Have dinner—"

She abruptly spun around and pressed her fingers to his lips. "I can't," she said. "I mean…" What should she say? That she was leaving the state in three weeks? That there wasn't time to build a relationship, so why start? "Oh, God, I'm horrible," she murmured to herself.

He gently pulled her hand from his mouth. "Service-oriented industry, remember? Whatever you want is fine."

"I doubt this was exactly what the janitor's union had in mind," she returned drily.

He let go of her hand to stroke her face. It was a soft caress with the pad of his thumb as he swept past her mouth up along her cheekbone. And damn if she didn't lean into the caress because it was just so wonderful. She searched his expression, the warm chocolate of his eyes were completely open and non-judgmental.

"It doesn't have to be dinner," he said. "There's coffee upstairs in the robotics lab. Or ice cream sundaes down the street."

"I'm leaving," she abruptly confessed. "The state. In three weeks. I don't want to lie to you—"

He kissed her. It was swift, it was deep, and it was thrilling. His hands delved into her hair to cradle her head, his tongue thrust into her mouth. She arched into his attack, trying to tease him with her tongue, and loving that he took control. He was powerful, her Elevator Man, and she reveled in it.

Within seconds, she was as hot as she'd been before the elevator doors had dinged open. Good God, she was insatiable! "This is nuts," she said against his mouth.

"I know," he agreed, as he obviously forced himself

to slow down. A moment later, they were looking at each other, their mouths apart, but everything else entwined.

"The thing is," she said, struggling to put words to the feelings colliding within her, "I've been working so hard for a really long time. Not only at my business, but before that, just to make it to Chicago to start."

"You don't have to explain anything," he began, but she shook her head.

"I need to. You need to understand. It's been going badly for a while now. We've fought hard, but it didn't work. We're going to have to close."

She saw sympathy warm his eyes. "That's why you're leaving," he said.

She nodded. "But then, wham, there's you two months ago. No talking. No work. Just desire. And suddenly I feel good, you know? I'm not thinking about work or bankruptcy or anything. Just you and me."

"Bodies without pressure." He released a rueful laugh. "I understand. Believe me, I get it."

"I don't want to lie to you," she said. "I just want to feel good for a while. Like I'm on top of the world."

He let one of his hands slide down. Within a moment, he was gripping her hips, pulling her gently forward to press against him. God, he was just as hot and hard as she'd remembered. As she'd lived and breathed in her fantasies for two months now.

"I'm okay with feeling good," he said. "No connections, no relationship. In fact, that's exactly what I want right now."

She took a deep breath, amazed at her own boldness. "I have condoms in my purse."

"I've got some, too," he said. Then he slowly touched her chin, tilting her face up toward him. "I've got a clean bill of health, and in case you're wondering, I've never done this before either."

Relief flooded through her. He could be lying, but she didn't think so. "I'm clean, too." She didn't say more. Just looked into his eyes while her heart beat faster and faster. She saw his nostrils flare and felt his body tighten as he slid his hand into her hair to cup the back of her head. She didn't think it was possible, but he suddenly felt bigger to her, stronger, more demanding. It was exactly what she wanted from him and she willingly gave herself over to it.

Their kiss was explosive. He thrust his tongue into her, exploring every inch of her mouth. She surrendered to him, opening herself up as never before. With other men, she was always thinking. What did that kiss mean? What did she want? Where was their relationship going—did he fit into her life plans?

But there was no thinking this time. She knew there was no future between them. And with that worry gone, her mind surrendered to the joy of the experience. Sam's kiss was all about pleasure, and she wanted to live every moment.

They toyed with each other for a while, their tongues tangling, their mouths fused together. Before long, Julie found herself impatient to touch him. She pulled at his T-shirt, trying to work her hands beneath the soft cotton. He let her, and her fingers soon slid across the rippling planes of his abs. And while she was glorying in the exquisite feel of his body, he gently backed her against the wall.

She hit the paneling with a soft thud, made all the better because he was pushing between her thighs, his penis rubbing her just how she liked it. Then he kissed down her neck, and opened her sweater again. Her nipples were tight, her skin so sensitive to the slightest brush of his thumbs or lave of his tongue.

He teased her left breast with his tongue, sucking it into his mouth where he nipped at it. She bucked at the incredible sensation and was startled to find that he'd already undone her pants. The fabric was drooping off her hips, and she pushed them the rest of the way down. Now that the rules were established, she was not going to hold back. She wanted him inside her. So she lifted his face, her breath too short to say much.

"Condom," she gasped out.

He grinned and hooked his hands behind her thighs. As he straightened up, he lifted her as well. Not far, just enough to perch her bottom on the railing as he wrapped her legs around his hips. Perfect! She got to watch the play of muscles across his chest as he twisted slightly to pull a foil packet out of his back pocket. A moment later, he'd popped the button on his fly and his erection sprang free.

He was big, just like she knew he would be. And while he fumbled with shaking hands to open the foil, she was able to touch him. She measured the length of him, stroked the velvet head, even rolled her thumb across the bead of moisture and wondered what it would be like to taste him.

She didn't get the chance. He touched her wrist, stopping her motion. "You wanted pleasure," he rasped. "That's going to shorten it for both of us."

She nodded and let her hand drop away, enjoying the sight of him suiting up. And again, she marveled at how easy this was. Her blood was humming, her heart was beating so fast, and a gorgeous man was moments away from fulfilling a fantasy she'd dreamed a thousand times. It didn't matter what had gone on earlier in the day. Failing business or not, this moment was perfect. Absolutely perfect. She smiled and was startled to find him looking at her, his eyes a dark chocolate mystery.

"What are you thinking?" he asked.

"Nothing," she answered. "That's the whole point."

He seemed to take that at face value as he slowly leaned in to kiss her again. She met him halfway, enjoying the feel of his lips, the play of his tongue against hers and the way his hand slid down her belly to the cotton of her panties. Then she broke the kiss, gasping at the shock of sensation as his thumb rolled over the fabric to stroke her clit.

"I've always wanted to do this," he said.

"Do a woman in an elevator?" she asked.

"Nope," he said with a grin. "This." He brought his other hand up to the edge of her panties. She watched in surprise as his forearms bunched and the elastic snapped. A second later her underwear was in shreds and he tossed it aside. Julie bit back a gasp while a silent thrill shot down her spine. So, okay the clothing had been old and probably easy to tear, but it didn't matter. The sight of his muscular arms ripping away her clothing sent her libido into overdrive.

"You are so hot," she murmured.

"I was just about to say the same thing," he said. This time, nothing barred him from stroking his thumb over her clit.

Her legs tightened and her back arched. And soon, oh God, please let it be soon, she was going to feel more than just his fingers. She was so enthralled with the idea that she began to move against his thumb, rhythmically circling around his hand.

"There's so many things I could do to you right now," he murmured.

Yes! She thought. Anything. Everything!

"Three weeks," he said in an almost conversational tone. "No dates. No relationship."

"Yes," she said. Those were her terms.

He nodded as he shifted his hips, positioning himself. "I'm good with that," he said. Then he finally, wonderfully, thrust deep inside her.

She groaned in delight as he filled her. She was impaled, held pinned—and half lifted—on his cock, and it was perfect. In fact, she had to lift her knees up along his hips to accommodate him. Never had she felt more thoroughly possessed.

Then he began to thrust. Powerful, deep, masterful penetrations. The rhythm was slow at first, but strong enough to feel all the way to her spine. She gasped at every slide. She arched her back, letting him go deeper, wanting to feel as if he completely filled her body.

And then the pace increased.

Her belly tightened. Her orgasm burst through. She came in a wave of pleasure. And still he thrust into her, pushing her even higher. Harder. Stronger.

Then, suddenly, he slammed forward as he convulsed inside her. Shudders wracked his body, adding to her pleasure. She gripped him tight, wanting to feel every pulse of his orgasm.

Oh, God! Yes!

SAM SLUMPED TO THE SIDE with a groan. He didn't so much intend to move as simply not fall over. How had this miracle happened to him? he wondered vaguely. No ties. No awkward relationship issues. Just the hottest sex ever. For three more weeks.

Thank you, God!

Julie was stirring by his side. He opened his eyes to

see her stretch languidly as she slid off the handrail and stood. She was still wearing her black heels, and wasn't that the greatest sight ever? Then she smiled at him, her eyes all vague and misty, and he rapidly changed his mind. *That* was the most gorgeous sight ever.

"You're so damn beautiful," he murmured.

She dimpled prettily at him. "I feel like I just swam in a lake after a long, long drought."

"I feel like I drowned in that lake," he countered.

She arched a brow and the expression was mischievous. "Well, perhaps I can give you a little CPR."

He released a laugh which was really more of a gulp for air. "Give me a minute. I'm pretty sure that the dead will rise again."

"I think…" she said as she stroked her hand across his chest, "…that I'll wear a dress tomorrow. Something with a swirling, flowing skirt. And really high red heels."

"It's alive!" he cried. And yes, the thought of Julie in a flirty dress with red stilettos had him fully resurrected.

She laughed as she glanced down at him. There was coy flirtation in her gaze, but he also caught a flash of anxiety. Then she turned away to pull up her pants.

Worried, he straightened up from the wall. "Julie…" he began, trying to think of something to ease the awkwardness. "I know this is unusual for both of us, but that doesn't have to make it weird."

"I know," she agreed. "And it was great. Really, really great."

"Yeah," he echoed. But then he didn't know what to say and she flushed and looked away. He went back to putting himself to rights, while she readjusted her sweater. Within a moment, she had everything tucked, hooked and tied back in place. Except for the slightly flyaway lift to her hair, she looked every inch the business professional. If it weren't for her torn panties on the floor, he might wonder if he'd imagined the whole thing.

She must have seen him glance at the plain cotton. "Oh," she gasped as she reached down.

"I got it," he said. And he did. He grabbed them before her, balling them tight then stuffing them into a pocket. He didn't allow himself to think about how depraved that was, grabbing and keeping her torn underwear. "So," he murmured. "You're leaving in three weeks."

"That's when my lease here is up," she said.

He swallowed, a tightness forming in his belly. It might have been anticipation, but he didn't really think so. Three weeks didn't seem like long enough. He'd built up seven weeks' worth of fantasies about this amazing woman. But that was all the time she had. She was leaving the state.

"Right," he said, though inside he begrudged the very idea. "A dress tomorrow."

"And red heels."

He arched a brow and attempted a wink. "I can work with that."

She winked back. It was a quick movement, almost unnoticed because she was turning away from him. But he saw it and he liked it. A woman who winked. And then she pushed the Stop button back in. Except, of course, the elevator didn't move. His phone was in control of the lift.

She pulled the button out again, then pushed it back. Nothing happened. "So," she said, "how do I start the elevator back up?"

"Hold on." He'd been scanning the area for his phone, finally sighting it on the floor next to the first glass panel. He picked it up and thumbed it to life. A few taps later, the elevator hummed into motion.

"And here I thought it was the Stop button," she said, her voice laced with humor.

"You have no idea how hard that was to arrange," he returned.

Her musical laugh was the last thing he heard before the doors dinged open on the garage floor. She stepped out. He would have followed but she stopped him.

"No need," she said, pointing to her beat-up Camry. "I'm right over there."

She didn't want him following her. He dipped his head in acknowledgment, but he still thumbed the app on his phone. The elevator froze open.

"I'll just wait here to make sure you get into your car okay." He shrugged. "I want to be your only stalker tonight."

She nodded again, and he saw relief in her expression. "Thanks."

Then she turned away and crossed to her car. He watched her the whole way, waiting until her car pulled out of its spot and drove down the ramp.

Three weeks. There was a lot he could do in that time. But only if he got busy right now.

5

JULIE PIROUETTED IN HER apartment. There was almost no room between her bed and the walls, but she did it nonetheless, loving the feel of her skirt swirling out from her legs. In truth, this was a spring dress meant for being flirty and fun. Bold white-and-red flowers covered the light cotton material. It was definitely not intended as a work outfit in the fall. But she paired it with a severe red jacket—which made it warm enough—and do-me red pumps which made it perfect for her promise to Sam.

She stopped her spin, and her skirt twisted back down around her legs. It took only a moment for the fabric to settle, but it took her mind a lot longer.

Was she really doing this? Was she really going to have hot office sex without thought to a relationship? To the man?

Yes! Or rather…maybe. After all, she did know something about Sam, even if she was trying to pretend that he was anonymous Elevator Man. Beside the obvious physical attributes—tall, strong, pecs of steel and extremely nimble fingers—she knew he was thoughtful enough to bring condoms and make sure she got to her car okay. She knew he was employed at a regular job, and that he had the sexiest smile—half challenge, half predator. When they'd met in the elevator—not just last night, but for the last seven weeks—he'd been there looking for her.

It wasn't PC. From one light, she could think of it as creepy. Except that she had invited him to stalk her. She had wiggled against him, let him touch her breasts, and then shared a great deal more long before last night's events. And boy was last night an *event!* God, she'd never orgasmed so intensely or so long in her life!

And then there was that *other* moment. It was bizarre, but she couldn't forget when he'd looked at her face, touched her cheek and said, "You're so beautiful." It sounded like a line, but it hadn't felt like one. His eyes had been wide, as if he were looking at her for the first time, and there had been surprise and awe in his voice. Awe. For her!

If only she had the time to get to know him better, to find out if they could have more than just hot times in the hallway. But the minute she thought that, she mentally shied away. She wasn't looking for a relationship. In fact, she wanted the polar opposite. She wanted a distraction from her life, from the fact that her glorious foray into big-city advertising had ended in inglorious defeat. Web Wit and Wonder had failed. All that was left was to gather up her broken dreams and go home.

Under those circumstances, who wouldn't want a wild, meaningless fling in the elevator? Especially if it resulted in orgasms that went on forever! But she couldn't forget that it was only a distraction. That as fun as it was to wear do-me heels and a flirty skirt, she still had to cancel her accounts, close up the office and pack up her things.

Her eyes teared at that thought. She couldn't even bring herself to look at her cell phone. She had to call her parents. She had to tell them she was coming back home and ask if she could sleep in her old bedroom. She had to confess to all and sundry that little Julie with the big dreams was really only suited for writing hardware store ads and sale announcements for the quilting society.

Her step was a lot less jaunty as she left her tiny apartment. By the time she had made it to her Camry, though, she was thinking of other ways to drum up business. Was there more marketing work somewhere? Their company was web based, specializing in internet advertising. But maybe there some print work to do. Maybe someone would hire them for newspaper advertising. By the time she pulled into her spot in the garage, she had to sit for ten minutes jotting down a list of places to check and things to do. If it weren't for the click of her heels on the garage floor, she might even have forgotten Sam.

She glanced at her watch. She was behind her usual schedule because of the extra time she'd taken to dress. The elevator doors swooped open, and she quickly scanned the interior. He wasn't there. Just three men in business suits and one jeans-clad engineer from the robotics company. The sight of his faded denim and loose tee made her flash on Sam's attire last night and she smiled. Then she was surprised as the engineer gasped and colored all the way up to his ears.

Oops. Apparently, thinking sexy thoughts had made her into a walking sex kitten. She consciously toned it down, turned a blank face to the closing elevator doors, and tried to think about her to-do list. If nothing else, that would sober her right up.

But she couldn't do it. Instead, her mind wandered over what she and Sam had done in this very elevator. Weirdly, she didn't linger on the waves of ecstasy, but on the moments leading up to orgasm. There was power in his voice. Or maybe the better word was self-assurance. As if he daily commanded people to do things, and they automatically obeyed. She certainly had. Sure he'd made jokes about being in the service industry, and he certainly dressed the part of building maintenance, but truthfully, the job didn't fit the feel of the man.

Sam had a strength about him, a confidence in his ability to arrange the world to his choosing. She responded to that power in him. She liked that he was masterful and that he had chosen to master her.

The elevator doors slid open and she had to walk down the long hallway to her office suite. The place was well lit, the security cameras hung discreetly high. It was one of the reasons she'd picked this building. The security was first-rate but still unobtrusive. So unobtrusive, in fact, that she usually forgot all about the cameras.

But she looked at them now with new eyes. Was Sam using them to watch her? Was he sitting in his coveralls, his large hand wrapped around a coffee mug, while he followed her on some monitor? The very idea gave her a little thrill.

She glanced up and down the hallway. At the moment, there was no one here. Very well then. He had left her high and dry in the elevator this morning, perhaps she'd get a little revenge. She walked until she was in perfect alignment with the camera nearest her office door. Then she "accidentally" dropped her purse.

She took her time leaning down to pick it up. She bent from the waist, keeping her legs straight and her butt high. The camera would have an excellent view of her bottom, long legs and do-me pumps. And then, when she picked up her purse, she let the edge of it catch the fabric of her skirt. As she lifted up the bag, her skirt went with it.

She waited a moment, straightening equally slowly as she pretended to root in her purse. Inch by inch, her full thigh was exposed to the camera. It went all the way up to the edge of her thigh-high hose and the red lace garter that matched her do-me heels. Then she pretended to discover her mistake. A shift and a wiggle later, and her skirt fluttered back down in place. Show over. Except for one thing.

She twisted to look directly up at the camera and winked. Then she strutted—yes, strutted—her way into her office. Sure, she had a mountain of details to mow through. Sure, she had a daunting pile of bills and a tiny pile of possibilities. But for this moment in time, she felt silly sexy. Who knew flashing a security camera could be so much fun?

SAM STARED AT THE MONITOR, his morning coffee forgotten amidst the press of his sudden, rock-hard erection. He'd meant to just glance at the monitors. He'd meant to drink his coffee, wait for Julie to get to work and then prepare his notes for this morning's meeting. Nothing earth shattering.

He hadn't counted on her doing a bend and wiggle right in front of the camera. How had she known he'd be watching for her? He'd been doing so for weeks. She'd never before given any indication that she even knew the camera was there.

Well, she had now! And he had the boner to prove it. He pressed the button to rewind the recording. He shouldn't torture himself, but he couldn't stop. In super-speed, she backed up out of her office, retrieved, then dropped her purse, then backed into the elevator. Another button push and she was moving forward again, this time in slow motion.

Step. Step. Pause. A glance at the camera. Right there was when she'd figured him out. And then…the show.

Oh, God, she was even more glorious in slow motion. And what was that on her creamy thigh? He froze the image and zoomed in. Red lace. His mouth went dry and his hands clenched with the need to touch her. He was going to drag that lace down her leg with his teeth!

"Welcome to the depressing Thursday report," Roger said as he sauntered into the lab.

Sam slammed his hand down on his keyboard, instantly shifting the screens to CNN. He'd tied his personal bank of computers to the security system after his very first elevator encounter with Julie. But that didn't mean he wanted to be caught peeping by his CFO. His Everest-sized hard-on was a little more difficult to hide, but he swiveled in his chair and pulled in tight to his desk. Let the paper-strewn monstrosity cover his own monstrosity.

Pasting on a fake bleary-eyed look, he peered over his coffee mug at his best friend. "You really ought to find a better way to greet your boss this early in the morning."

Roger was undeterred. Dressed in a gray suit, red power tie and Italian leather shoes, he grabbed a lab stool and hauled it over. But he didn't sit. Instead, he snagged a rag and wiped off the metal spinning disk before gingerly setting his briefcase down on it.

"I've got reports, more reports, and then just for fun, some paperwork for you to sign," he said as he pulled out thick packets of stapled papers. "All of them say one thing: I do not like this economy."

Sam snorted. "I don't think you're alone in that."

"We've got to do something about it."

"The whole economy?"

"Just our little slice of it." Roger pulled a black pen out of his pocket and passed it to Sam. "Sign here and here and here."

Sam frowned and reached up to the huge, lighted, magnifying glass that swung above his desk. It was meant for people to use when doing detailed circuit board work, but Sam needed it for more than just that.

"Why don't you get glasses like a normal person?" Roger asked.

Sam started scanning through the pages. "I have contacts."

"That need reading glasses instead of that huge monstrosity."

"This is bigger. Can't lose this or sit on it," he responded as he flipped a page in the contract, doing his best to concentrate as he read.

"You're a multimillionaire," Roger groused. "You should get stylish lenses that make you appear sophisticated and—"

"Geriatric."

"Better than a doofus."

Sam didn't answer. He had a rare eye condition that left him visually impaired. Fortunately, technology and medicine had advanced enough that he could read a monitor and see distance objects with the aid of hard contact lenses that reshaped his eyeballs and magically filled in the ripples in his cornea. Close-up work, however, required a shift in magnification or a different pair of lenses. That was one of the reasons why he'd first started working on circuit boards so long ago. Everyone needed to use a lighted magnifying glass to do that, so he hadn't felt handicapped.

Right now, he had on his distance lenses so he could watch Julie on the monitor. That meant he needed help to read the contract. Instead of reading glasses that made him feel like an old man, he chose to use the massive wall-mounted contraption that made him look like an engineer.

Sam sighed and scrawled his signature on the appropriate lines, then leaned back in his chair. He had to get his mind off of Julie and back onto his company. "So, do you really have Thursday-morning depression to report? More than a general I-hate-this-economy?"

Roger swooped up the signed contract and popped it into his briefcase. "Sadly, yes. We're not selling enough robots."

Sam pushed the magnifier away so that he could focus on his friend's face. "We don't sell robots."

Roger grimaced. "You know what I mean."

They didn't sell robots like what people imagined. R2-D2 or C-3PO weren't in their catalog. RFE sold robotic attachments to other things—wheelchairs, prosthetic limbs, even low-end laptops. That was why he'd named the company Robotics for Everyone. The problem was insurance didn't always pay for what they provided and potential customers either couldn't afford what they offered or didn't know the products existed in the first place.

He'd made his initial millions on a wheelchair attachment to help customers get in and out of custom designed vans. It was still his bestseller in part because the van manufacturer did all the marketing for him. But Sam's recent products were less easily marketed. They needed their own publicity to reach potential customers.

"What does Ginny think?" Sam asked, referring to their head of marketing.

"That she needs help."

Sam's thoughts immediately went to Julie and her advertising company. He could hire her. He could keep her in town. He could—

But it wasn't that easy. He needed big dollar advertising including television and major print. From his research, he knew she did brilliant work in internet ads, click-through campaigns, and some cool animation, but was very thin on television experience. And he already had a huge advertising firm under contract. He couldn't just stuff her into the mix because she winked at a camera and melted his higher brain functions.

Which meant his company still had a problem. He grimaced as he looked at his best friend. "You don't have a depressing Thursday report. You want me to do a corporate powwow to figure out how to generate more revenue."

Roger gave him a thumbs-up. "You got it in one!"

"But I've got a ton of work to do." And a woman in red heels waiting to be seduced.

"You can't work if the company goes belly-up." Roger abruptly leaned forward, flipping through one of the reports to point to a specific table. "Do you know what you spend on R & D? In one month alone?"

"Research takes money."

"Not corporate R & D. You, Sam. You alone in this lab."

"I am the corporation, Roger," Sam said, irritation lacing his tone. "I am the one who designs the projects, has the vision, makes all this happen. I work how I work."

Roger sighed and pulled over another stool. It was a measure of how serious the situation was that he didn't bother to wipe the seat down first. "I know that, Sam. We all do. And if you say no meeting, then we'll all happily go back to our cubicles."

"You have a huge office with windows," Sam groused.

"But we need a breakthrough," Roger continued. "And not of the genius engineering kind."

Sam toyed with a stack of extra-large circuit board prints on his desk. He rubbed his thumb over the corner edges and pursed his lips. "That is not my strength," he muttered.

"But you are our fearless leader. So suck it up and lead."

Sam sighed, knowing his friend was right. "Fine. Gather the troops. I'll be there in ten."

"Stop acting like it's a firing squad. We need inspiration."

Sam shot his friend a dark look. "I said fine. I'll be *inspirational* in ten."

"Good." Roger stood and left. Sam didn't see if he did his usual mock salute. He was too busy flipping his monitors back to the hallway outside of Julie's suite. Roger wanted inspiration? Sam couldn't think of anything more inspirational than a view of Julie. Unfortunately, she was safely inside her office and blocked from his camera's prying eyes. So he tapped some buttons and pulled back up the recording of her morning purse drop.

Indulging himself, he expanded the view and slowed the display. Then he leaned in close and allowed his whole vision to be filled with the creative, dynamic woman he'd been stalking. Damn she was a beauty, and not just because she was physically pretty. She was, of course, but he was drawn to her energy and her joy.

He knew that her company was closing. That she was leaving because her business had failed. And yet she did not seem defeated or diminished. Far from it. The woman on his monitor was *alive,* and that was damn sexy.

Well, he thought, as he reluctantly shut off the connection to the security cameras. He certainly had his tasks cut out for today. Task 1: get a brilliant marketing strategy to save his company. Task 2: create a seduction scenario worthy of a woman in garters and red stilettos.

Fortunately, he'd spent half the night working on Task 2. The program he'd created was already up and running, but he'd set it for a morning scenario. This morning was now occupied, so he would have to delay until this afternoon. Switching to his laptop, he pulled up the program. A few keystrokes later and he'd set it to detonate at 3:00 p.m. It would be hell waiting that long, but Julie was more than worth it.

6

JULIE WAS DOING PAPERWORK in a sauna. That's what she was thinking as she waved her hand in front of her face to create a breeze. What the heck was wrong with the heating vent? It had been pumping out roasting air better designed for an oven than an office suite.

Karen knocked then sauntered in with a few more pieces of paper which she added to the pile on Julie's desk. "Found a few more receipts."

"Thanks."

"No problem. I'm really here just to admire your new look."

Julie flushed. With the out of wack thermostat, her crisp sundress had been wilted down until it was barely there. No jacket. No bra either because it had become too confining after 2:00 p.m. She didn't tell Karen this, but she'd also pulled off her thigh-highs and her underwear. It was too hot to wear hose. She'd left the garter on, though, mostly because it made her feel sexy. And sexy was a way better feeling than depressed, given that she was doing accounting.

"I've called down to maintenance," Julie answered,

ducking the question of her change in attire. "They swear they're working on the problem."

Karen shrugged. "It just seems to be your office. Mine is fine." And Karen did indeed look crisp and cool in her dark jeans and artistically patterned top. "You could come join me in my room."

"And be buried in charcoal dust? Thanks, but no." Karen was a genius at animation and a variety of digital arts. But she did all her rough work in charcoal first. Said it gave her a more hands-on feel. Whatever the reason, Karen's office had charcoal bits everywhere, which would naturally attach to every inch of Julie's skin. "Your artist space is your own. And my sauna of hell goes great with doing accounting."

"Any leads on new jobs?"

Julie swiveled to tap her computer to life. "Nothing new. And since the internet went out fifteen minutes ago, I'm stuck with balancing spreadsheets for now."

Karen grinned. "Better you than me!"

"Hey, do you mind—"

Pop! The power died.

"Son of a—" Julie rapidly began tapping keys. She had battery backup on her laptop, but she'd been working all afternoon on these spreadsheets. She didn't want to risk losing anything.

A moment later, she released a sigh of relief. No problem. Everything was safe and sound. The surge protector had done its job, the battery was working fine, and except for the fact that her office was lit purely through the window, everything was hunky-dory. *Not.*

She grabbed for her cell phone to redial maintenance, but stopped when she heard Karen gasp in surprise. Julie looked up to see her friend shift to the side and right behind her stood Sam, her very own Elevator Man.

He was wearing his coveralls, which looked relatively clean. But that was about all of him that appeared fresh. His mink-brown hair was shot every which way, his eyes appeared tired, even from this distance, and there was a general slump to his shoulders.

"Wow," Julie blurted out as she put down the phone. "You look like you've had a day and a half."

"At least," he said tiredly as he hefted his toolbox. "But it's starting to look up."

Karen gestured him into Julie's office. "Well, it's a good thing you're here because I think she's starting to melt from the heat."

"Internet died about fifteen minutes ago and now…" Julie gestured to the lights. "Well, you can see that we just lost power."

"Freaky," he drawled, and damn if she didn't catch an undertone of something. Julie narrowed her eyes at him, but his expression remained completely neutral. Meanwhile, Karen had stepped behind the man's back, but remained in view as she pointed to Sam and mouthed the words, *Is that him?*

Julie felt her face heat. She hadn't told her friend about last night's exploits or their plan for the next three weeks. But Karen knew that Elevator Man worked in the building and wore coveralls. It was a good guess. And, of course, she was absolutely correct.

Julie nodded as discreetly as possible while Sam bent down and began rooting through his toolbox. Karen arched her brow, obviously inspecting the man's tush, then gave Julie a big thumbs-up.

"Find those receipts," Julie chided. "If you want the business to refund you, then you gotta get those receipts."

Karen huffed. "Okay, okay, I'll keep searching. I

know the hotel bill's in there somewhere." Then she shot Julie a mischievous grin. "Want me to close your door?"

"No," Julie returned with a stern look. "It's too hot in here for that."

Sam lifted his head. He held his cell phone in one hand and some electronic gadget in the other. "Maybe I could re-route the air vents. Give me a moment."

Unable to resist, Julie arched her hands over her head and lifted her hair off the back of her neck. That accentuated her cleavage in the front of her dress, plumping it nicely, as she gave off a breathy sigh. "That would be heavenly."

Thankfully, Karen was back in her office, so she didn't see the display. Julie kept her eyes cracked open just enough to see if she'd had any effect on Sam.

Sadly, the answer appeared to be no. Though he was looking in her direction, his gaze seemed to be too vague to be centered on her cleavage. If anything, she would guess he was listening hard. To her?

"It'll take me a moment to find the problem," he said. "I'm going to have to crawl around a bit."

Julie released her hair with a deflated grimace. "No problem," she said in her normal voice. "I'm just sitting here pretending I'm an accountant." She tapped a few keys, bringing her laptop back to life. "You'd think it'd be easy to say 'zero balance,' but apparently, the IRS wants things itemized."

Sam was over by the wall, carefully pulling aside a bookcase. His forearms bunched with the effort, but that was all. Otherwise, he appeared completely at ease with the weight of dozens of books. Damn, she liked a strong man.

"Is the money the problem or the accounting?" he

asked, his attention shifting to a wall panel he'd now exposed.

"Both," she answered as she pulled up the spreadsheet. "And it's especially tedious if you wait months to enter all this crap."

"Procrastinator, huh?" he said as he raised his gizmo and starting punching keys.

"Only for things involving numbers. Me and math have never been friends."

"I always liked getting it right," he said. "So much else in life is vague…" He waved his hand in the air. "There's a solidity in two plus two always equaling four."

"Or two minus eight equals debt," she said, more to herself than to him. "Me, I'd prefer some vagueness to that statement."

He chuckled at that. "So how'd you end up in advertising? I look at you and I think beautiful actress or world-famous artist. Not something as prosaic as web marketing."

She leaned back in her chair, unsure how to respond. "I don't know. I've just always known who to go to and what to say to get what I wanted."

He arched his brow. "Something tells me you were an alpha girl in high school."

She shook her head. "Not really. But I knew what to say to get their attention. I knew how to get them behind the Humane Society garage sale, for example. And where they went, the football players did, too."

"Bet the event was a huge success."

"It was. Five years running," she said, remembering the flush of her first big success. "It was all a matter of the right pitch to the right people."

He laughed. "A born marketer."

"Maybe. But raw talent only gets you so far. I took a ton of advertising classes in college and got my business degree with a marketing focus." She gestured to the other office. "Karen's the genius designer. Give her a half hour and she can create a kick-ass web page for you. But she needs me to tell her what to say to which audience. She can make it look incredible, but I'm the one who makes it hit the right notes."

"Sounds like you two make a good team."

She sighed. She'd thought so, too. Too bad the real world hadn't been as kind. Stuck in her morose thoughts, she didn't notice at first that he'd fallen silent. He wasn't even tapping on his gadget. But eventually she forced herself out of her gloomy thoughts to look at him.

"Something wrong?" she asked.

"Hmm? Oh, no. Just, um, gonna have to crawl around a bit more." Then he hesitated a moment. "You know, the robotics firm on the top floor is looking for marketing help. Maybe, well, maybe you should look into it. Perhaps there's something you could do for them."

She frowned at him, thinking hard. "RFE? The mega-firm upstairs that owns the building?"

He nodded. "You'd have to talk to the head of marketing. Her name's Ginny Smithson. Maybe you can work something out."

Julie plopped her hand on her fist, thinking hard. "I'm probably too small-time for them."

"Yeah," he said a little too quickly. "I shouldn't have mentioned it. Shouldn't have gotten your hopes up."

She flashed him a quick smile. "I live on hope, Sam. And a lead's a lead, right?"

"Yeah, but don't put a lot of effort into planning a pitch—"

She held up her hand to stop him. "It's fine, Sam. I'll

figure it out. Thanks." She grabbed a pen and scribbled Miss Smithson's name down. She needed to do some research into the company, get a feel for what they did and what they might need. Working up a proposal would take a lot of hours, and to do it right she'd need graphics and a good idea. But she could try, right? She had three weeks.

She spun toward her laptop. "Any chance you could resurrect the internet?"

"I'll need to check into your router, but at least I can get us lights." He tapped a key, and sure enough, the lights came back on.

"Great," she drawled with a disgusted sigh. "I can read more bills while I wait for internet."

He chuckled. "And, you know, it is really hot in here. I know it's not standard uniform, but would you mind if I, um…"

"Unzipped your coveralls?" she finished for him. "Feel free. Take them off, in fact."

"Thanks." Then he flashed her a smile that made her think twice about what was going on. He looked part devil, part cat-ate-the-canary. Had she just walked into one of his schemes? She'd been so deep into work mode that she hadn't really been thinking sex. Of course, she hadn't *not* been thinking it either, what with Elevator Man right here. It was just hard to switch gears.

But now that she'd seen his smile, and the way he looked at her as he placed his hand on his zipper, her belly was starting to tighten with anticipation. It had been a hell of a depressing day already and it was only a little after three. She deserved a distraction, right? Anything was better than accounting. And hot sex was a thousand times better than anything. Though, she wasn't exactly sure what they could do with her door open and Karen in the office right beside hers.

Meanwhile, Sam started unzipping his coverall, taking his time as he faced her. "I, um, was planning on working out after work. It's pretty much all I do. Work and work out."

She arched her brow. As the heavy coverall fell aside, she saw a tight muscle tee beneath. Simple cotton, torn sleeves, but clingy enough to reveal every ripped inch of his torso.

"Are you sure you don't mind?" he asked. Then he paused, shooting her a significant look. "I can come back later if this is a bad time."

And there it was. The message that this was indeed something he'd cooked up, or maybe it was simply a situation he wanted to take advantage of. Either way, he was asking her if she wanted to play. Right here, right now.

The answer was yes. A thousand times, yes! She'd been working hard, and just the sight of Sam standing there with a devilish gleam in his eyes made her go liquid with desire.

"Um, no," she said, trying to keep her tone light. "This is the perfect time."

"Good," he said as his gaze dropped to her cleavage. Right on cue, her nipples tightened and her skin heated to a rosy flush. Then he grinned. "Don't tell my boss I'm doing this," he said as he pushed the coveralls down off his lean hips.

"I won't tell a soul," she murmured. And that was the last coherent thought she had as she took in his body. He was wearing biker shorts. Long, lean, black Lycra that outlined everything, and she did mean everything. There he stood in glorious, tight-assed, corded thigh detail. Her gaze slid to his front, but there was padding there, so he just looked huge. As in godlike.

"You must work out a lot," she said in a thick voice.

"I have a stationary bike I use when I can't sleep."

She arched a brow. "Can't sleep much?"

"You have no idea," he drawled.

But she did. She couldn't sleep much either, especially when she lay in bed fantasizing about him.

"Well," he said. "Let's see what I can do about your internet problem. Where's your router?"

She swallowed. "Under my desk. Right over here."

His smile was slow and sexy, and his eyes told her that he'd known exactly where the router was. And that she was going to enjoy every moment of whatever he had planned. "Great," he said, his voice low and sexy. "Go back to work. I won't bother you at all."

She sincerely doubted that, but that was part of the thrill. He was pretending this was work like normal, that everything was businesslike and professional. Her heart started beating triple time.

Meanwhile, she had to play her part. She dutifully turned back to her spreadsheets. She had a large L-shaped desk. Her laptop sat on the short end of the L, while piles and piles of paperwork were stacked along the extra-long side. And beneath that stretch of desk was her router, a ton of wires and Sam in a muscle tee and tight shorts as he crawled beneath.

"Hey, Julie, I didn't find the hotel receipt, but I unearthed these." Karen rounded the corner, waving a sketchbook and papers. "Whatever happened to this campaign?"

Julie twisted back to the longer part of her desk. She was excruciatingly aware of Sam doing who-knew-what to the electronics right beside her feet, but she did her level best to keep her expression straight as she held out her hand to her friend.

"Which campaign?" she asked.

Karen handed the sketches over, but her eyes were scanning the room. She tilted her head toward Sam's toolbox and mouthed, *Where is he?* Thank goodness his coveralls were crumpled behind the bookcase out of sight, otherwise the question might be a lot more specific. As it was, Julie could only point down to the floor and write on a nearby pad. "Internet router."

Karen waggled her eyebrows which Julie did her level best to ignore. Then she started to open the sketchbook. It was a good thing that her hands were occupied because at that very moment, she felt a hand on her calf. It was Sam, of course, stroking the back of her leg with his large hand. It took everything in her not to gasp. Or purr in delight. As it was, all she managed was to stare blankly at the sketchbook.

"Julie?" Karen prompted.

"Hmm?"

"You're staring at a bad sketch of a monkey."

Julie blinked and refocused on the page in her hands. "I'm just trying to remember which campaign this was for."

"The zoo."

"Oh, right." She might have said more, but at that moment, she felt Sam's lips on her ankle. His fingers were doing wonderful things to her calf, too, massaging away aches she didn't even know she had. "Oh right. Of course," she babbled, rapidly scrambling for something to say to Karen. "Weren't we going to use it for something else also?"

Sam gently cupped the back of her calf and pulled her

leg forward. Her heel left the ground and he tugged her foot to the side, spreading her legs beneath the desk.

"Well, there were a ton of Chunky Monkey jokes."

"Right. Haha." Sam's hand was now flowing up over her knee to touch the inside of her thigh. Julie's internal muscles clenched involuntarily and her toes curled. What would he do when he discovered her garter?

"Wait a moment!" Karen abruptly cried.

Julie froze. She'd die if her friend figured out what was going on beneath the desk. Sure she'd wanted to be a wild woman, but only in private.

"There was another campaign," Karen continued. "Hold on. I'll be right back." She spun on her heel and dashed out of the room.

That gave Julie a moment to readjust. She was about to tell him to cool it while Karen was still here, but she didn't get the chance. Right when she was about to push away from the desk, she felt something cold circle about her ankle and click into place.

Click?

Sure enough, another click closely followed the first. Julie tried to pull back to look, but her ankle was abruptly brought up short. What the heck?

She twisted to look down. There was Sam, his eyes glittering with mischief right next to the handcuff he'd attached to her desk leg. The very same cuffs that also surrounded her ankle. The man had just handcuffed her to her desk!

She stared down at him, her mouth dropping open with shock.

"Here it is!" called Karen from the other office.

Sam held up a finger to his lips, motioning for her to be silent. Julie had no choice but to agree as Karen came back into the room brandishing a stack of printed designs.

"Monkeys for the day care bid. Remember?"

"Oh, yeah," Julie said weakly. That's all she could manage as Sam returned to stroking her leg. Higher and higher he traveled on her body, his long fingers brushing up past her knee. He was about to discover the garter, and Julie was tight with anticipation. What would he do when he found that?

Meanwhile, Karen was flipping through pages, pointing at this and that. "That was one of your better ideas. Good caption, good ideas."

"Um, yeah." Her nipples were tightening as Sam slowly worked between her legs. Was she really doing this? Was she letting a man tongue his way up her body at work? With Karen right there? Oh, God, she was. And she was loving it! "We...um...worked hard on that."

Karen straightened. "She said she'd get back to us next month with a decision. Maybe you could call and prompt her?"

"Already did." Julie was feeling heat roll across her skin. Her nerves were tingling, her legs relaxing open. It was getting hard to focus. "She, uh, hasn't decided yet. And, you know, it's not enough money."

"Oh." Karen visibly deflated. "Not enough money to pay the rent? Or not enough to pay our current bills?"

Julie extended her hand, tapping her laptop as she pretended to think. The motion had her spreading her legs even farther and her breath shortened at the thought of that. What she was doing was scandalous, appalling, and absolutely wonderful. He was touching her, stroking her thighs, kissing her skin and completely taking her mind off work. And bills.

"Julie?"

"Both," she answered, her mind splintering as Sam finally found the garter. "I mean neither." His fingers toyed with the lace, slowly tracing it to deep between her thighs. Meanwhile, she gave her friend a helpless shrug. "It's just not enough money."

And that's when Sam's fingers finally got deep enough. With her movements above desk, he had managed to spread her legs wide. And now his questing fingers realized she had stripped off her underwear in the heat. She was commando beneath her skirt. Apparently it was a big surprise because he jerked in reaction, banging his head on the underside of her desk.

"Ow!"

Karen blinked. Obviously, in her excitement about the day care campaign, she'd forgotten that Sam was even there. Not a problem for Julie. Doing her best to act casual, she dropped her head enough to see under the desk.

"Everything okay down there?" she said, her voice laced with humor.

"Everything's peachy," he returned as he looked at her. One hand was rubbing the top of his head. The other was steadily working its way back between her legs.

She shouldn't have allowed it. Certainly not with Karen standing right there. But he was touching her, and she liked it. So she didn't fight it, and in the next breath she felt his fingers on her mound. A moment more, and his knuckle was pressing deeper, sliding down between her folds. Oh sweet heaven, it was great.

"Well, um, it was a thought," Karen said absently, her mind obviously still on the campaign.

"And a good one." A shiver was traveling up her spine. He was opening her up beneath the desk, spreading her legs even farther, and using his long fingers to touch every part of her.

"I'll go look for that hotel receipt."

"No problem," Julie answered as she passed back the sketchbook and designs.

And Karen finally left her office. Good thing the temperature had been wacko in her office, otherwise her friend might have noticed the sweat glistening on her skin. Julie was just taking a deep breath of relief when she felt Sam push her skirt up to her belly. And while she gasped in reaction, he wedged himself between her knees. She didn't know how he managed it. He was a big guy and there wasn't a lot of room beneath her desk. But he was there, and now her legs were spread as far as they could go.

"Sam!" she hissed.

He looked up at her, the mischief in his eyes unmistakable. "Just checking the wiring, ma'am."

She didn't know what to say. She ought to tell him to stop. There was anonymous elevator fun, and then there was this. With Karen right next door! But then he started kneading her thighs, pressing his thumbs in deep enough that the muscles just gave way. She let out a sigh and yet she couldn't stop a worried look at her open office door.

"We've both had hard days," he said against her skin. "And we're going to go back to them in a moment." He tongued her thigh. "Just relax and let me check your router."

God, he was persuasive. She let her eyes drift shut as she enjoyed his caresses, his tiny kisses along her thighs, and the slow, thrilling shift of his fingers to her core. Before long, she was tightening her bottom, lifting herself up as his thumbs began to stroke her.

She couldn't stop herself. She tilted forward on her chair, sliding herself closer to him. His mouth couldn't get to her, but his fingers—damn, he was good with his fingers. Random circles, long leisurely strokes, everything she wanted and yet not enough.

"I give up!" Karen called as she came around the door again.

"What?" Julie strangled out the word in shock and horror. It was terrible and incredibly erotic all at once to be this close to orgasm and not be able to show it. Her belly was quivering, her nipples ached, but she couldn't touch herself. She couldn't touch Sam! All she could do was look up at Karen with as close to a bland expression as she could manage.

"Yes," Karen huffed from the doorway as she rooted in her purse. Thank God! The woman wasn't even looking at her. "I'll never find that receipt. And I want to get home anyway before the traffic gets nuts."

"Oh," Julie said weakly. Sam had slowed his movements, going for long strokes that kept her simmering without toppling her over the edge. "So you're going home now?"

"Yes," Karen said with a sigh. "But I swear I'll be back tomorrow. We will live to fight another day!"

Sam began a series of steady, incredibly arousing strokes from her core to her clit. Oh, she was in heaven and hell all at once.

"Um, hey, Karen," Julie managed. "Would you mind shutting the door? I think I want to cry in private." Cry, scream, come all over Sam's hand.

"Sure thing, sweetie. See you tomorrow."

No sooner had she heard the soft click of the door pulling shut than Sam went into overdrive. He hooked her uncuffed leg over his shoulder, giving him more room beneath the desk. She squeaked in alarm, but she didn't dare give full voice to it. Karen might still be in the outer office.

"I've been dreaming of this all day," he said as he began to nibble around her garter. "Ever since you flashed me this morning."

So he had been watching her in the camera. The idea made her grin. And then she gasped, her hips bucking in shock as his thumbs rolled over her clit. He took advantage of her movement to slide his hands under her bottom. She was now completely cupped in his hands.

"All damn day," he muttered as he used his teeth to pull her garter down to her knee. Then he stopped to flash her a grin. "Finally I can get a really good look at your wiring."

7

SHE CAME. Sam would have grinned if he weren't occupied with holding her down as she writhed against his lips and tongue. He held her as long as he could manage, wanting to prolong her pleasure—his pleasure—because damn if it wasn't the hottest thing on the planet when she went wild.

But in the end, he lost his grip. Or rather, her chair slid out from under her and she tumbled to the floor. He caught her, keeping her from hurting herself. But he couldn't do that and keep her orgasm going, so he chose safety over pleasure. And then discovered that it was its own kind of pleasure to hold her while she lay panting in his arms.

In time, her breath eased, her body changed to completely boneless, and her lips curved into a dreamy smile.

"Mmmmm," she said without even opening her eyes. "Feel free to come fix my router anytime."

He chuckled as he stroked a lock of hair from her cheek. "I'll keep that in mind."

"Nope," she said. "No mind. No thoughts. Just… this…floating…yumminess."

He looked at her face. He was at the right distance to see it clearly. He saw the smudges of exhaustion beneath her eyes and the faint lines on her brow. They were almost smooth now, but he would bet anything that they'd furrow up again the minute she went back to work.

"It's bad, isn't it?" he asked, though he knew it would break the mood.

She cracked an eye at him. "Um, no. It was great. It was…" She chuckled. "Orgasmically fantastic."

He smiled at her joke. "No, I mean your company. What we're doing here…" He gestured to her stretched out on the floor, her legs still splayed and her skirt rucked up to her belly. "It's because everything else is so bad, isn't it?"

As he feared, her expression sobered. She took a deep breath and pulled her legs together. He helped her, twitching her skirt down to cover her thighs, though he mourned the loss of the view.

"Let's not talk about that," she said, her gaze skating away from him to grimace at her desk.

"But maybe I could help. If it's just a temporary setback—a cash flow problem—then…"

"Stop!" Her hand shot up in the air. "That's not what this is," she said firmly. "We… You… It's just—"

"Temporary relief," he said when she couldn't find the right words.

"Of the absolute best kind," she added with a grin. Then she extended her hand to touch his cheek. "You're sweet, you know, offering me money. But you don't know how deep in the hole I am, and I wouldn't take it anyway."

"I have more money than you think," he said softly.

Probably millions more than she thought. After all, she still believed he was a maintenance worker.

She shook her head. "It doesn't matter. Ten cents or ten billion. I'm not taking it." Then she rolled toward him, her expression going mischievous. "Nice touch, by the way, handcuffing me to the desk." She rattled her ankle for emphasis.

"Nice segue away from the topic."

She shook her head. "Nope. Just a return to the primary task." She propped her chin on her hand. "You just fulfilled one of my dark and horny fantasies."

"Sex under a desk?"

She nodded. "Yes, I'm depraved."

She said it so lightly that he laughed. As far as depraved went, that was pretty tame.

"But," she continued, "I don't want this to be one way." She reached out, startling him by cupping his full length. The heat of her hand seared through his bicycle shorts, but that was nothing compared to the pressure. Damn, she had such good hands. "Love the outfit, by the way. What exactly possessed you to wear it?"

His shrug stopped halfway as she started to stroke up and down the length of him. He abruptly pulled her hand away or he'd come right there.

"I was the chubby, half-blind kid in school. Couldn't see well enough to do anything athletic."

She straightened up. "Half-blind?"

He nodded. "Congenital eye thing. Even with contact lenses, I often have to use glasses. My goggles are even prescription." He gestured to his toolbox. His goggles were right on top.

"I'm sorry," she said. "That must have been hard." There was no pity in her voice, and his heart warmed.

"It was harder on my brother. He's completely blind.

At least I can see, thanks to modern technology. And my sister's eyes are completely normal. But for Tommy, well, we're still far away from cybernetic implants."

She frowned. "Isn't the robotics firm working on something like that? I heard it on the elevator, I think. Couple of engineers talking about helping the blind to see."

Sam felt equal parts surprised at her knowledge and nervous about his identity. It was ridiculous given that he'd just offered her money. If that wasn't a clue that he was more than he pretended, then he didn't know what was. But he also realized that he liked her thinking of him as a regular Joe—or rather regular janitor—because they could relate to one another as people without the pressure of his image as a millionaire mogul.

"Um, yeah," he hedged. "They're beta testing a kind of radar that gives sound cues when things are close. But it's really complicated and too expensive for the average person."

"That's too bad," she said, her brows narrowing. "I bet you know all the good gossip in this building. Given the security around here, you probably know who's sleeping with whom, who's cheating on their taxes, who could benefit from a good ad campaign..."

Not hardly, but it was a good guess given that he pretended to spend his days watching her on the security monitors. "I know some things," he hedged, "but nothing about advertising." But he knew someone he could ask. Maybe the *real* head of maintenance would know.

She smiled. "It's okay. That's my job anyway, not yours. Though it occurs to me that I might be just one in a whole harem of elevator conquests."

He laughed. "No, I swear. You're the only one to see me in my bicycle shorts in years."

"Yeah, back to that…" She pushed up so that she was sitting beside him. "Seems a strange thing to wear to a handcuffing…er, anklecuffing."

"I wanted something sexy that would work under coveralls. This was all I had. Don't even own a pair of regular shorts."

"So you're a jeans or Spandex kind of guy?"

He snorted. Put like that, he sounded gay. Or like someone with a superhero delusion. "You're making me feel like that fat ten-year-old again."

"Oh, no," she purred as she ran her hand up his thigh. He stopped her before she got very high, but it didn't seem to matter. Her voice sent his dick into overdrive. "The look definitely works on you. Or rather, on me."

All his blood had pooled south of his brain, but he wasn't completely stupid. "You don't want to go back to work, do you?"

She lifted her hand so that she could stroke up his chest. Her fingers were cool across his belly, but his blood heated nonetheless.

"Don't underestimate yourself," she said. "You don't look chubby or blind. You look ripped. And hot enough to keep my mind off of bills for a very, very long time."

"Julie—"

"I'm still cuffed to my desk," she said when he might have backed away. Clearly she had no interest in deeper conversation. "The bondage must mean something to you. Do you perhaps have a domination fantasy? Are you the big, bad boss, and I your worker slave?"

He swallowed. Damn, she did have a good imagination.

"Oh, my," she said in a high, anxious voice. "What must I do, sir, to gain my freedom?"

He didn't really have a domination fantasy. Unlike the janitor he pretended to be, he was boss over scores of people and had no need to prove his power to anyone. And yet, she was obviously enjoying herself, having fun with her role-playing fantasies.

Unable to resist, he waggled his eyebrows at her. "I don't know, Miss Thompson. You have been quite the slacker lately. Taking naps under your desk and all."

She grinned even as she ducked her head. "Ooh, I don't know. Maybe I need to be spanked." Then she lifted up on her knees enough to twist her bottom toward him.

He nearly swallowed his tongue. "Are you seriously up for spanking?" he asked, incredulous. He'd never been interested, but the sight of her pert little behind made his dick twitch.

Meanwhile, she was obviously thinking hard. "I… uh…I don't know," she finally confessed. "I'm just beginning to explore my wild side. Whips. Leather. They're all possibilities, I guess." Then she leaned down close to him and her hair slipped over her shoulder to tickle his face. "You're the one who cuffed me, Mr. Bossman. What do you want to play?"

God, she was delightful. No one ever asked him to play. Not Mr. Robotic Billionaire. Not since he and Tommy had been kids. And no one but Julie had ever looked at him like that, playful and seductive all at once.

"My god," he whispered, stunned by the realization. "I've forgotten how to play."

She laughed, the sound high and sweet. "Life been too

serious for you, Elevator Man? All broken thermostats and power outages?"

More like circuit boards, way-too-expensive AI components and failed marketing plans. But he didn't say that. All he did was nod dumbly at her. "That's why I first noticed you, even before our, um, collision in the elevator," he said as much to himself as to her. "You were laughing. I remember the sound so clearly. You sounded like you were having so much fun."

She looked at him, her expression slowly sobering. They were nearly nose to nose. One little shift forward and he could kiss her. But he didn't. The mood wasn't right. It wasn't sexual—or kissing kind of sexual, at least—and she was obviously thinking hard.

"Poor Mr. Elevator Man," she said softly. "Half-blind and working in the basement all day."

The top floor, actually, but the effect was the same.

"You don't even go biking for real, do you? Just stay on an exercise bike." She shook her head. "You gotta get out of this building."

Unable to resist, he touched her face. "Come with me. Make me laugh like you were that day."

He saw her think about it. He saw her look into his eyes and bite her lower lip. Then her eyes zipped sideways to her desk.

"The bills will be there tomorrow," he coaxed. "You're worried about me, but when was the last time *you* got out?"

She twisted her lips into a half smile. "I got *off* about ten minutes ago."

He smiled. "Not the same thing."

"What would we do?"

"Whatever you want."

Her eyes narrowed, but there was a gleam of excitement in her gaze. "When was the last time you went bowling?"

"Wii bowling? Or normal?"

She blinked. "Uh, normal." Then her eyes widened as she figured it out. "Wii bowling can be made huge on the screen. Normal bowling…"

"Not so much."

She frowned. "You'd kick my ass at Wii bowling, wouldn't you?"

He smiled. "Maybe." Definitely.

"Normal it is then."

"What? Wait a minute!"

She shook her head. "How bad are your eyes? Can you see the pins? They have lines in the lane, and the real secret to bowling is in the hands anyway." She leaned forward until her lips were almost touching his, teasing him as she spoke. "And you've got great hands."

He wanted her right then. He wanted her more than his next breath. But he didn't want to break the magic of this moment either.

She must have understood. Either that or she was simply a mind reader because she pushed up to her feet with a sigh. "Problem is, I'm still chained to my desk. I don't know if my boss will let me free."

He stayed still on the floor, looking up the long expanse of her leg and that loose, flowing skirt. Worse, he knew that she had no underwear on beneath.

"Bend over," he rasped. "Bend over like you did this morning."

She twisted slightly, looking down over her shoulder at him. And then—yes!—she winked before she slowly, delightfully bent at the waist.

"I have something in my purse," she said as her skirt

slowly inched up her thighs. Her bottom was right in front of him, and he touched it, stroked it through the soft cotton of her dress. God she was perfect, he thought as he got to his feet behind her.

"Here it is!" she cried. "Maybe this will buy me my freedom." Still bent over, she offered him a foil packet.

He took it, his dick so hard it was painful to move. But he didn't want her to feel obligated. Like the only way he would take her bowling was if she spread and presented, so to speak.

"We don't need to—"

She straightened enough to shoot him a glare. "You stand there like my own personal sex god and are refusing me? That is so not fair!"

He gaped at her, but she didn't give him time to speak.

"Yeah, I'm being blunt here, but workaholics like me don't have time to beat around the bush. You're the one who chained me to my desk. You're the one with the sculpted abs and the big hands. Now are you going to fulfill the promise of those tight shorts or am I going to have to drop a bowling ball on your foot?"

He laughed. God, he really laughed. But he did it while he was pushing down his shorts and suiting up with shaking hands. Meanwhile, she had widened her legs—and thank you, God!—she was still wearing those great red stiletto shoes.

"Miss Thompson, you have been a bad girl," he said sternly, getting into the spirit of the game. "I'm going to have to punish you."

"Oh, no, sir! I'm a good girl! I swear I am!"

He grabbed her shoulders and pushed her forward, moving her arms so that she was bracing herself on her desk. And then he slid his hands down her torso, taking time to fondle her delicious breasts.

She whimpered in mock horror, but she arched her back in clear invitation. And when he pinched her nipples, he swore she shuddered in delight. Then he slid his hands lower along her hips before abruptly flipping her skirt up over her back. There she was, all pink and perfect right in front of him. "Don't move, Miss Thompson," he ordered. "Good girls don't move."

Her eyes widened. "I'm a good girl," she whispered.

He slid his hand between her legs, stroking a slow circle over her clit. She arched into his hand.

"You're moving, Miss Thompson."

"I'm sorry," she gasped, clearly not sorry at all.

He pulled away, shifting his hands to her hips as he positioned her. "You cannot move, Miss Thompson. Do you understand me?"

"Yes, sir. I'll be still. I promise."

He put himself at her opening. He felt her muscles clench, even before he pushed inside.

He thrust hard into her, making her gasp and him groan. "You moved," he rasped. God, she wrapped him in hot, tight heaven. "You need to be still," he ordered as he pushed his hands under her dress, gliding upward until he cupped her breasts with both hands.

"Yes," she whispered.

He pinched her nipples once, and was thrilled when she shivered. "Yes, *sir*," he ordered.

"Yes. Sir!"

"Now, don't move." He withdrew, a slide that had his eyes rolling back in his head. She whimpered at the loss and tried to slide backward with him.

He pinched her nipples again, this time adding a tiny twist. "I said don't move!"

She froze in full arch. Her head was thrown back, her breasts were thrust into his hands, and her bottom was quivering. But she didn't move and he couldn't get enough of the sight.

"God, you're beautiful," he said as he reversed direction. He pushed in a little. Oh, it was torture. To hell with slow. He tightened his belly and rammed the rest of the way home. Yes!

"May I..." Her voice was high and breathy. Soft pants filled the room. "May I move a little, sir?" she asked. "One tiny part of me?"

"Since you asked nicely," he said. "You may move one thing."

He thought she was going to press against him. He thought she might push her breasts harder into his hands. He was wrong.

Her body remained completely still. Everything, that is, but her internal muscles. She squeezed him. One long full squeeze, then she relaxed. His breath caught in his throat. Never before had he experienced such a deliberate, controlled pressure. Not like that.

His hands clenched. Hell, his whole body clenched in hunger. "God!" he gasped. "Where did you learn that?"

"Tantric yoga," she answered. "I read. I practiced. But I've never tried it before." Then she twisted her head enough to look at him. "Can I move again, sir?"

He swallowed, fighting to keep his voice level and casual. "Yes, Miss Thompson. I believe I would like you to...oh, God."

She was doing it again and he was in heaven. One long, slow contraction.

"Miss Thompson," he said, his voice unnaturally thick. "I believe I was wrong. You are a very good girl."

"Thank you, sir."

"I think you deserve to be rewarded." He massaged her breasts. He was clumsy, his mind fogged with lust.

"Oh, sir!" she cried as he thrust into her. He hadn't intended to move, but his body was taking over, his need to have her overcoming all restraint.

He moved a hand down between her legs. Two strokes later, and she slipped over the edge. She cried out, arching into his hand. But it was the way she convulsed around him that sent him over.

He slammed into her, embedding himself as deep as he could go. It was like his mind detonated and his body was just part of the explosion. His consciousness went, too. Mind, body—everything—followed her into oblivion. And then...

His beeper went off.

8

JULIE LAY COLLAPSED forward on her desk, her orgasm still rippling through her, though in a muted way now. She mostly felt bliss in the quiet way of a silent mind, a pleasured body and a man still deep inside her. She'd never told anyone, but she felt pleasure just from feeling filled by a man. Orgasms were beyond great, but this was awesome, too. Penetrated. Impaled. Expanded. Whatever the word, Sam did it for her.

His beeper was a persistent buzz now, loud and annoying from his toolbox. Sam groaned as he lay on her back. He was pleasantly heavy, and his moan made her laugh. She didn't want him to move either, but she didn't want him to lose his job.

"Shall I get it?" she asked as she squeezed him one last time.

He slowly pushed himself upright. "You're going to kill me."

"But you'll die happy," she drawled. "I've heard that before."

"Doesn't make it any less true," he said. He slipped free and half walked, half stumbled to his toolbox.

Rooting around, he pulled out not his beeper, but some clean wipes. He offered her the container, and she pulled some free gratefully. He grabbed another for himself. Meanwhile, the electronic buzz just kept on going.

"Really. You gotta answer that."

He pulled up his phone and thumbed it silent.

"No, really," she said as she straightened up and her dress slipped neatly into place. There were wrinkles, but not too bad. It was one of the reasons she loved this outfit. "I don't want to get you in trouble."

He arched a look at her. "I think I'm already in way deep."

She didn't answer, her throat suddenly dry. His look and his tone suggested something other than getting into trouble with his boss.

She bit her lip, surprised that the idea didn't generate fear. Sam was a nice guy, and he was seriously hot. What would be the problem with moving anonymous fantasy to a more personal level?

She winced. The problem would come when she moved back to Nebraska in three weeks. "Sam..." she began, but was cut off when she tried to step to him. She couldn't. She was still cuffed to her desk. "Uh, you got the key handy, bondage man?"

"Maybe I want to keep you there—" His words were cut off as his phone buzzed again. He grabbed it with one hand while the other rooted about in his toolbox, then passed her a small key. She was freeing herself when he started cursing.

"Damn. Damndamndamndamn!"

"Crisis?"

"Disaster," he said with a heavy sigh as he tapped out a message with angry clicks. "Robotics lab. EMA caught on fire. Morons."

"Emma?" she asked.

"Hmm?" He was still thumbing through messages. "Environment Management Aid. Fancy robot for disabled people. The thing that costs about sixteen times what a normal person can afford." He dropped his phone back into his toolbox, his expression one of complete disgust. "Morons."

She raised her eyebrows, a little surprised to hear him so dismissive of people she knew must have impressive educational backgrounds. "I'm sure they thought they had it under control."

"So am I," he groused. "But they were wrong. I told them to make sure it didn't overheat. They assured me it would be fine. I assured them they had to triple check the specs. Apparently, they ignored me, and now I have to go clean up the mess."

She frowned as she lowered herself into her desk chair. "They're robotics experts. Maybe something else went wrong." She didn't say it, but her thought was, *you're just a janitor. How could you think you know better than the engineers upstairs?*

Except he'd been right. There had been a fire. And now, for some reason, he was the go-to guy for cleanup. His cell buzzed again and he turned it off, a look of frustration on his face. Then he started pulling on his clothing, his mind obviously churning. But about what? Fire cleanup?

"Should we…um…evacuate the building or something?" she asked. "Are the firemen on their way?"

He looked at her, a frown on his handsome face. "What? Oh. No. Fire's out. I just have to go make sure…" His voice trailed off and he flushed. His gaze canted away to his coveralls which he reached for with a grimace. "I've, uh, gotta go mop up the…uh…

extinguisher mess. A janitor's work is never done," he added with a wry twist to his lips.

She stood up and crossed to where he was pulling on his coveralls. With a smile, she brushed his hands away and zipped it up herself. Slowly. Carefully. Taking her time as she tucked all those glorious abs away beneath heavy cotton.

He watched her. She could feel his eyes on her face, even as she was looking at the broad expanse of his chest. And when the zipper was pulled all the way up to his chin, she finally lifted her gaze to his.

She wanted to say something. She wanted to express her joy, her complicated regrets about her future, and her simple thanks for the time they'd already shared. But she didn't have the words. So she did the only thing she could.

She stretched up on her toes and kissed him. Deep and full while his arms wrapped around her and pulled her tight. His mouth was masterful, dominating her quickly, just as she wanted. And just as she wanted, her mind slipped away beneath the onslaught. Her body tightened, her core went liquid, and in an instant she was hungry for him again. Forget the robotics lab. The real fire was right here between them.

He broke away from her with a groan. They were both breathing hard, and he hadn't released his hold on her.

"I want to see you again," he rasped. "And not just for this." He tightened his hold on her, pressing his full erection against her. Wow, he was a man with a quick recovery! "I want to go bowling with you right now."

She grinned. Really, it was the greatest turn-on to have a guy this hot desperate to be with her.

"You need to go take care of the robotics lab. One of

us should have a paying job." She said it with a laugh, but then immediately sobered. She did not want to suggest that they were a couple. That one of them should be working to help cover for the other.

Thankfully, he didn't seem to notice her mistake. He stepped away from her and rubbed his hand over his face in frustration. "I don't know how long this thing is going to take tonight. What about tomorrow night? Wanna hand me my balls tomorrow?"

She snorted at his double entendre. The things she wanted to do with his balls did not involve a public bowling alley or special shoes. But that, of course, was the exact problem. This whole thing had started as fantasy sex play. Going out together was taking it to a whole new and personal level.

Sure, she'd been the one to suggest it in the first place, but now—after the glow had faded—she worried about what she was doing.

"Sam," she began, choosing her words with care. "I'm leaving Chicago in three weeks."

"I know—"

"And I don't do long-distance relationships. They don't work."

He paused for a moment, his eyebrows narrowing. "You mean, it didn't work, don't you? You tried it once with someone and it didn't work that time."

She shrugged to cover her surprise. He was a perceptive man. "High school sweetheart. Jerk was unfaithful at college orientation, but I didn't find out until Christmas."

"That sucks."

She nodded. "I sobbed all through the holiday. Fortunately, I met jerk number two right after." Her lips curved in a semblance of a smile. "We did have some good times there for a bit."

"And then?" he prompted.

"Then he took a year abroad. I pined for him nightly."

"And he was tripping the night fantastic down the Champs-Élysées?"

She nodded. "But it was a Tokyo street and a French exchange student."

He winced in sympathy. "Ouch. I never kept a girl-friend long enough to go long distance. We always broke up before we moved apart."

She took a deep breath, half wanting to know more, half shying away. "The point is," she said with a sigh, "I'm leaving in three weeks."

"You keep saying that—"

"Because I *am*. This was never intended to be more than—"

"An elevator lay. Yes, I know." His voice was curt, his expression tight with frustration. Then he moderated his voice and his face as he touched her hand, gently twining her fingers with his and tugging her closer. She didn't move, so he stepped closer to her.

"I know this is your wild fling before leaving. I get that. I'm okay with that." He didn't sound okay with that, but she didn't argue. "But it doesn't have to be all fantasy, right? We can still go bowling, can't we?" Then he leaned forward, touching his forehead to hers. "You said I needed to get out more. This was your idea."

"I know! And you do!" she huffed, abruptly torn. She wanted to go with him, but she also didn't want to dig in deeper relationship-wise. "But shouldn't you be looking for other girls? Other friends?"

He laughed, but the sound came out strained. "How

'bout I take a small step at a time? One night out with a girl who is designed to *not* be long term. Then, after she goes, I'll think about someone else."

She wasn't fooled. He was angling for more time with her. A deeper connection. And truthfully, part of her really wanted that. He was funny and sexy and kind. And when she was with him, she didn't think about the bills on her desk or that she hadn't told her parents she was coming home in ignominious defeat. Sam made her smile. And scream in orgasmic frenzy. Why wouldn't she want to go bowling with him?

"It's short term, Julie. I get it. Just say yes, so I can go save the building from overeager robotics engineers."

She laughed and the word came out along with her giggle. "Yes." Then she stretched forward and kissed him lightly on the lips. "Yes. But only to get you out of this building, Mr. Lonely Elevator Man. And only because I need the ego boost of trouncing someone at something!"

He smiled. "Beat me any time at anything." Then he held her hips and ground playfully against her. "In any way."

God, he knew just how to tease her. "Tomorrow at six, we'll go for the three Bs."

He tilted his head. Three Bs?"

"Beer, brats and bowling. What, haven't you ever been in Nebraska?"

He tilted his head. "Not in recent memory."

"Well, I don't know if it's a tradition *everywhere* in Nebraska, but my family is a big Three-B fan."

"I look forward to learning the wonders of Nebraskan traditions."

She arched a brow. "Look forward to getting your

butt whooped at bowling, Elevator Man." Then she waved. "Now go! Save us from burning alive."

He nodded with a grimace as he grabbed his toolbox. He paused a moment, clearly wanting to say something. She nodded in silent understanding. She didn't know what to say either.

With another nod, he moved to her door. She was already turning back to her desk when he stopped. She was listening to his every move, so she knew the moment he paused and she looked up, wondering what he wanted.

"Sam?"

"Your internet's back up. And the thermostat's fixed. You shouldn't be having any more problems."

She took a moment to feel the air. He was right. The temperature was back to normal, the electricity absolutely stable. She knew if she tried it, her internet would be fine.

"Was it ever really broken?"

He flashed her a cocky grin before he left. He hadn't answered her question, but she already knew the truth. He had engineered everything that had happened here this afternoon.

Damn, the man was innovative! That he had turned his prodigious skills to fulfilling her fantasies was an amazing stroke of luck. How had she managed to hook up with the one guy who could stop elevators, super heat her office *and* play bossman games? Her face heated at the memory. And then she started thinking about what new and special fun he would cook up for her next.

It was only after she'd returned to the bills, after she'd opened her laptop and started looking at accounting numbers, that her mind raised the obvious question. It was a small question, but it nagged at her. If Sam could do all that, plus tell engineers where their robot was going to go wrong, what was he doing as a janitor?

TWO-FIFTEEN IN THE MORNING and Sam was staring at his email. His eyes were bleary—even more so than usual—his pet project EMA was a charred mess, and he needed a shower really bad. But here he was at his desk, his gloved hand hovering over the Send button.

Did he dare? Did he take the risk?

It was an invitation to Miss Julie Thompson of Web Wit and Wonder to visit the CEO of RFE to discuss potential work. It wasn't from Sam, the Elevator Man. This was a formal invite to discuss a possible job. It was a lure that Julie would surely grasp with both hands. And it was a big damn lie.

There wasn't work at RFE for her. Well, maybe there was. He didn't know. He'd have to talk to Ginny about that—but that wasn't the point! It was the coward's way of forcing him to come clean to Julie. She would accept the invitation because she was desperate for work. She would come up here all professional and energetic, ready to pitch whatever her creative, brilliant mind came up with, and then she would see him.

She would know he was not some janitor. She would realize that he'd been lying to her all this time. And she would…what? Be angry? Definitely. Hopefully, he could get her past her anger, but then what? Would she forgive him? Maybe. Would she turn on him and try to extort a job out of him? Maybe. That was, after all, exactly the lure he was using to bring her up here. He couldn't blame her if she did.

But then what? An office romance? Just like she didn't do long distance, he put the kibosh on dating people he worked with. He'd had a couple relationships with coworkers, and all had gone up in flames. One of them had even taken a corporate project with her when she left.

He did not want that happening with Julie. But he couldn't keep being her janitor, either. Yes, he'd said he was okay with three weeks of anonymous sex, but that was a lie. A big fat whopper of a lie.

He wanted more with her. He wanted to spend time with her, to explore their chemistry—sexual and otherwise—for as long as he could. Three weeks or three centuries—it didn't matter. At the moment, he wasn't picky. He just wanted time to find out if they fit in more ways than under her desk.

But what if she found out the truth and called everything off? He'd barely managed to get her to agree to bowling. That was as personal as she wanted to get, and even that was a stretch. What if she found out who he really was and everything got very weird, very fast. And not in the cuffed-to-her-desk kind of way?

He sat down in his chair and pulled off his lab gloves with a grunt. Hell, was he really willing to risk ending hot forays into sexual fantasy for the possibility of a relationship? The possibility of a relationship that was likely going to end in three weeks? Was he nuts?

Yes. Yes. Yes. Completely bonkers. But he had to get closer to Julie. He had to meet her honestly as himself. Only then would they have the chance of progressing beyond the elevator.

With a sudden burst of courage, he hit the Send button. After all, he rationalized, he had just *proposed* a meeting, not set the time and date for it. They could get together later in the week, when he was more certain of Julie's reaction. Or, if things went badly at bowling, he could postpone the appointment until after she'd left for

Nebraska. He was just giving himself options. Confess or not. Meet or not. Hot sex or not.

His gaze traveled over to where replacement parts for EMA sat in pieces on his table. Robots were so much easier than women. Robots never made you sweat over emails. They never made you question your fundamental lifestyle, like if he had forgotten how to have fun or not. And they never, ever made you leave the lab.

Which was the whole point, wasn't it? That's why he had noticed Julie in the first place. She was bright and funny and so alive that he couldn't ignore her. She was the one thing that he would never find in robotic components. Which meant he had to take the risk. He had to do whatever necessary to make sure that he didn't chicken out.

Flipping through his calendar, he quickly composed another email. In it, he suggested James S. Finn, CEO of RFE, meet with Miss Thompson on Friday afternoon at 4:00 p.m. That way, if things went badly, they could separate without too much awkwardness. But if things went well, then they'd have a whole weekend to play. He paused a moment to think about exactly when was the last time he'd *planned* a weekend of play. Something that didn't involve reconstructing a robotic version of EMA. Not since he was a young kid at home.

He was smiling as he hit Send. "I'll just have to make sure that things go well," he said to EMA's robotic circuit board brain. "Very, very well."

9

THIS WAS A BAD IDEA. Sam had thought he needed to leave the office building, get out and spend time with Julie. That had been the idea and the reason he thought Julie was so appealing: because she forced him out of his comfort zone. And if that meant out of the building, then that was great. Except it wasn't great. It was terrible. And some comfort zones were not meant to be expanded.

"Something wrong with your brats?" Julie asked from where she was tucked up against the counter. Friday night at Great Balls Bowling was apparently the place to be for half of Chicago. They were currently at the alley bar for beer and brats, and he had yet to touch either.

"Huh?" he said, leaning close to hear. Mostly he was trying to get a good image of her mouth so that his specialty glasses could read her lips and transcribe what she said into a bright, white rolling screen of words that only he could see. But it was dim in the bowling alley. And noisy. And way too much for either him or his glasses to deal with. Hence the reason this excursion was a really bad idea.

"I asked if there was something wrong with your brats?"

Thank god he could hear because his software translated her question as: I donkey if sarong pong bras?

"Oh," he answered. "No, nothing's wrong." He dutifully took a bite of the thick, greasy sausage. Hmmm. Not bad. "I just didn't think they served brats at a bowling alley."

"My brother came for a visit my first year in Chicago. We called half a dozen places before we found this one." She popped a bite into her mouth. "Back home we would call these acceptable, but not Nebraskan."

He arched his brows. "Nebraska specializes in brats?"

"They do if you ask a Thompson."

He nodded. His glasses had translated that as: They do if you eat Adam's one.

"How long did your brother stay?"

"Just a weekend. He's in the navy. Was on the way to somewhere, but managed to fly in on Friday, hang with me, then continue on Sunday." She gestured out toward the crowded lanes that he couldn't see except as a blur of color and sound. "We came here that Friday. Then again on Saturday."

Sam caught an edge to her voice. Not a bad one. Just a hint of pride over the affection. "Let me guess. He beat you on Friday, but you kicked his ass on Saturday."

She released a bark of laughter, which his glasses read as: "Ow! Ow!"

"How'd you guess?" she asked.

He shrugged. "I am not unfamiliar with sibling competition."

She frowned. "You took pride in beating your blind brother in stuff?"

"Hell, yes!" he said. "He was a chess master by sixteen. And, yes, I also took great pride in beating my little sister, too. She thought about going pro in tennis but decided law school was the better choice."

"Hmm," Julie said as she set down her beer. "So you had a brilliant older brother and an athlete younger sister. Just how did you compete from the middle?"

"Very well, actually," he responded with a grin. Then he leaned in close as if to impart a great secret. Really, he just wanted to get close enough to smell her. In this place of noise and chaotic colors, his sense of smell was the only thing left, short of touching or licking her. Not that he was opposed to that either. "I had a secret weapon."

"Really?"

Hallelujah. His glasses got that one right.

"Yeah. I cheated."

"How?"

"Computers. Robots. Anything mechanical that could give me the edge. My brother was blind, so I bought the best chess program I could afford and let it play for me."

"Clever," she said, appreciation gleaming in her eyes. Clearly she understood the drive to best a brother.

"It worked for a while, but he found me out." He shrugged. "My sister ratted on me."

"Oh. Well, so how did you get back at her?"

"She was an athlete, and I couldn't see worth a damn. So, I used the only weapon I had."

"Which was...?"

"I hobbled her."

Julie snorted into her beer. "You put chains on her ankles?"

"More like weights in her shoes. Or her racquet. My favorite, though, was this wheeled robot that I put on her side of the court to 'help' her."

"You made a robot?"

He nodded. "It's not that hard, and my dad was an electrician, so he helped me set it up. All Bessy had to do was roll around at random and interfere with Janet's shots."

"Bessy? You named your robot Bessy?"

"It was perfect. She was huge, moved like a drunk cow, and was designed to Beat Sissy." He straightened in mock offense. "I was very proud of Bessy."

"And here I thought I had it hard just trying to protect my Barbies from three older brothers."

He nodded sagely. "Life was cutthroat at my house."

"Really?" She leaned forward, close enough (finally!) for him to smell her hair. But he only got a tiny whiff before she pulled back and he was once again overpowered by the scent of grease and stale beer. "I can't always tell when you're serious and when you're teasing."

"Teasing," he answered easily. "Actually, we're all really close, physically and emotionally. Well, except for my sister who has relocated to D.C. She's clerking for a federal judge."

"Nice!" she said, and he felt a surge of pride at her clear admiration.

"We're weird, but we're good people," he said honestly.

"Ditto for us," she said, and his glasses got that right, too. "Older brother in the navy, and a sister at home helping out. Well, still looking for exactly what she wants to do with herself. And littlest bro is in construction. He wants to be an architect."

"And mom and dad?"

"Nurse and football coach, respectively. You?"

"Mom's a disabled rights advocate and Dad's the electrician. Janet's clerking, like I said, and Tommy's a massage therapist. Owns his own company in Wilmette."

"And you're a janitor," she said slowly, obviously wondering how that happened. One sibling clerking for a judge, the other handicapped but running his own massage therapy business. A janitor just didn't fit the picture.

"Maintenance engineer," he corrected stiffly.

"But with clear understanding of robotics," she said. "Enough to tell the RFE geeks that their thing was going to catch on fire."

Sam stilled, his eyes widening. She couldn't possibly have figured it out, could she? She couldn't *know* that he was James S. Finn, could she? Ah, hell.

"Julie…" he began.

"Did you finish college?" she asked, her words accurately transcribed by the glasses.

"What? Um, yeah. Kind of." His mind was spinning with the fear that she'd discovered the truth and her question threw him.

"What does that mean?"

It meant that he'd poured his last tuition check into his first robotics product. The one that was the foundation of RFE. And that he'd only finished his degree years later through a special dispensation from the department. He submitted his design specs as a "special project" and got credit for taking a graduate seminar he'd actually taught. That arrangement had made his parents happy and Ginny thrilled because she could say he was a college graduate when RFE applied for research grants. Still, compared to some of his employees, his educational pedigree was seriously lacking.

"Um," he hedged, because Julie was still staring at him, expecting an answer. "I've thought about going back to school."

She shook her head. "I can't figure you out. You seem so smart," she said.

He snorted. "It's not like we've been doing calculus together."

"No, but not everyone can stop an elevator with a touch on their cell phone. And readjust my office thermostat and stop the power just to my office. And, by the way, thank God it didn't hurt my computer."

He waved a forkful of brat at her. "I sent a save message first through the wireless to your laptop. You wouldn't have lost anything. And I knew you'd backed up your entire laptop the night before."

She stared at him. "How could you know that?"

He squirmed, abruptly realizing he was talking too much. "Um, backups are a feature of our web service to which you subscribe."

"But my laptop—"

"Is backed up to RFE's. You're slotted for every Wednesday night."

She paused a moment, chewing the last of her brat in silence. Then she set down her fork and leaned forward. "Like I said, sometimes you seem scary smart. So why aren't you doing something more than fixing office thermostats?"

"I dunno," he mumbled. "Low self-esteem?" He couldn't look at her when he said that whopper. Feelings of low self worth were hardly his problem. In fact, his last girlfriend had accused him of having a god complex.

Julie, too, snorted in disbelief. "You seem rather self-assured to me."

He stiffened. "Sexual prowess is not the same thing as academic *cojones*." And truth be told, he did sometimes feel bad that he didn't have a PhD. But he didn't really think he needed one."

"What are you hiding from, Sam? And why do you keep fiddling with your glasses?"

"Huh? Oh." He pulled off his glasses, glad to have some way to distract her from the topic at hand. "They're an RFE prototype. Lip-reading software embedded in the glasses."

"No way!"

He showed her how to work the screen, then helped her put them on.

"Oh, ow," she said, flinching at how his lens prescription obviously distorted her own vision. "Uh. Wait."

Her eyes narrowed into a scrunch, and she played with the readout size. Once she was done, he pulled her chin over until she looked directly at his mouth, then spoke clearly and slowly to allow the software its best shot.

"Now look directly at my face. See how it picks up my words?"

"Oh! Oh, wow." Then she tilted the lenses down so that she could look over them at his face. "This would be so cool if only it worked."

He grimaced. "Didn't get my words right?"

"Not unless you just said something about elephants and freeways."

He pursed his lips. "That's exactly what I said. I said, look, there's an elephant on the freeway."

"Well, then I'd say all that other stuff about looking at your face came up wrong." She tugged off the glasses and handed them back to him. "So you're walking around with an RFE prototype."

Sam shrugged. "I'm friends with the owner."

"Speaking of which, I got an email from him today."

"Oh?" he said as nonchalantly as possible.

"Yeah. Seems he wants to talk to me about a possible job. Wonder how that happened."

"Like I said. I'm friends with the owner."

She tilted her head. "So how come you can ask him for a job for me and not one for yourself?"

Sam almost groaned. His lies were starting to get complicated. "First off, I don't know that there's a job. I, um, he just wants to talk to you. Discuss possibilities, if there even are any. And second, I already have a job."

She shook her head. "Something doesn't fit."

"Yeah," he bit out, way more irritated with himself than with her. "Me. And I never have."

He pushed up out of his seat and rooted into his pocket. He couldn't read the bill, so he just slammed down a couple of twenties. That ought to more than cover their tab. Meanwhile, Julie was scrambling to her feet.

"Sam! Wait!"

He turned away from her, self-disgust souring in his stomach. He'd meant to impress her tonight. He'd meant to sweep her off her feet with his charm. Instead, he'd piled lie on top of bad lie, and they hadn't even gotten to the disaster that would be him and a bowling ball. And his glasses didn't work! At the moment, the waitress appeared to be saying: Frog water cartoon. Best nail. Sam reach up and switched off the glasses, forcibly restraining himself from throwing the damn things across the room.

Meanwhile, Julie had grabbed her purse and made it to his side. "Sam, talk to me. What's going on?"

"This was a bad idea," he snapped. "I thought it would be good for me. That you would be good for dragging me back into the world."

"Why is that a bad idea?"

"Because I'm not a normal guy, Julie." How did he tell her that the rare times he went out, it was with the mayor of the city or to some benefit dinner? "I'm just not what you think," he said miserably.

"Is it the vision thing? Is it really that hard to see?" she asked as she gently tugged on his arm to pull him out of the main path. "I'm so sorry. I didn't think about how this would be for you."

He sighed, grateful she had given him a convenient excuse for his churlish behavior. But it was still another lie. "It's just gotten complicated," he tried again. "You didn't want a relationship, so it was easy to pretend I'm something I'm not."

"When was the last time you left the building, Sam? You're seriously upset here, and I figure it's because you usually stay home, and order in. Am I right?"

He nodded. She was right.

"And you probably spend a lot of spare time tinkering with your friend, Mr. Finn of RFE. Trying out funky glasses that don't work."

"Uh, yeah," he said. "And, for the record, it's the lip-reading software that doesn't work. The glasses are just fine." They weren't really. He could see clearly from about a foot in front of him to ten feet. Beyond that, it was all just a flashy blur.

"Right," she drawled. "In short, you lock yourself

away because of your eyes. In fact, from the sounds of it, I'd say your blind brother probably gets out more than you do."

He couldn't argue with that. His brother was quite the playboy up in his wealthy suburb of Wilmette. In fact, Tommy's favorite saying was that all the best things were touched, not seen. And stroked, and fondled.

"Oh, look!" Julie said before he could relay that little tidbit. "Our lane's up." She started tugging him forward, but Sam refused to budge. He pulled her back around to face him.

"Julie, we need to talk."

She arched a brow. "I don't care if you gutter every time, Sam. You're going to go bowling. It's not about the score. It's about you trying something outside of your comfort zone. Just try it."

"No, Julie, you don't understand—"

"Listen to me," she said as she shifted around so that her face filled his lenses. If the translator was still on, she would have given it the best angle for use. As it was, she gave him a full view of arched brows, smooth skin and her determined jaw.

"Getting out of your cave wasn't a bad idea. It was a great idea."

"Let's go back to the office," he said. "We can be private there."

"We'd just end up playing more sex games. And yes, that's awesome, but you're the one who wanted to get to know me better." She touched his face, her fingertips so gentle they were in direct odds to the firmness of her voice. "Look, if you're really about to melt down, then we'll go. But you don't seem hysterical so much as uncomfortable."

"I could descend into hysterics if you'd like."

"Don't think so," she said, though her lips twisted into a smile. "Don't limit yourself, Sam. Just have fun, that's all I ask. We don't even have to keep score."

"I'm not worried about the score," he said. "A ten-year-old could probably kick my ass." In fact, his sister had routinely beaten him physically from when she was seven.

"Stop worrying about your performance," she said. "You've been an uptight mess since we got here, and not because we're about to bowl. You started getting anxious when we were just talking."

What could he say to that? She was right. Aside from the whole lying thing, he hadn't realized how much he liked being in control of his surroundings. He had everything exactly how he liked it in the lab. And when he went out, it was as James S. Finn, mega-millionaire. He rode in limos and went to exclusive restaurants. Now he was in a bowling alley trying to impress a girl, but unable to reach for his usual bag of tricks. It was exactly what he wanted, and yet, it bothered him, too. How childish was that?

"Come on," she urged. "Just try to relax. Give it a good faith effort, and if it doesn't work, we'll leave."

"Promises, promises," he muttered, but he allowed her to tug him forward.

She laughed, the sound ringing out over the clatter and roll of the nearby lanes. "Make it through an entire game, and I'll give you a reward." She gave him a mischievous waggle of her eyebrows.

"That better be one hell of a reward," he groused, but his tone was good-natured.

"I guess you'll just have to bowl to find out."

He groaned. A reward from Julie could be quite an inspiring thing. Especially when she winked at him just like she had on the security monitor the day before. Hell, he was already going hard thinking about it.

"Fine," he said. "But if I bowl straight into someone else's lane, it's your fault, not mine."

He followed her laughter to find their assigned alley. Then she put a ball in his hands, walked him up to the lane and said, "Go get 'em, tiger!"

"Julie—"

"Oh right!" she said, shifting his body position. "The pins are that way."

"I can see them well enough, Julie," he said. "I just wanted to say, thanks. This *is* good for me. And it's even better that I'm with you."

Her face softened into a misty-eyed smile. But then she shook her head. "Nice try, tiger, but we're not leaving no matter how sexy you are. Now bowl!"

He laughed, feeling his chest ease with the motion. Then he began his motion. A real ball wasn't anything like a Wii remote, but he knew the concept. Three steps, a swing and release. Not a big deal. Especially if he focused on the arrows on the wood pointing down toward the pins.

Three steps. Swing. Release. Then he cringed in horror when someone screamed.

10

JULIE WHIPPED AROUND at the scream. She found the idiot immediately, two lanes over. Someone over there had made a strike and she apparently thought it was a terrible thing or a great thing or the girl just wanted to make noise. Whatever the reason, it had obviously spooked Sam. He was hunched over, trying to scan the crowd, a worried frown on his face. Finally, he looked desperately at Julie.

"Did I kill someone?"

"Nah," Julie drawled. "She's just a screamer. You have that affect on women."

"Oh." His shoulders visibly relaxed. Then he squinted down the lane. "Gutter ball. Hell."

She shrugged. "Want me to tell you why or should I save your male ego?"

"Hm. Tough choice." Then he heaved a dramatic sigh. "But I suppose I'll go for the unvarnished truth. But give it to me easy. I'm frail, you know."

No, he wasn't. At least his body wasn't. And as for his ego, she was still deciding about that. If he really did have a tender ego, then he wouldn't be here in the first place, wouldn't be caught dead doing something that he couldn't win at. At least not against her. But then there was that whole question of why a guy who was obviously smart was working a dead-end job in building maintenance.

She leaned forward, trying to see exactly how fragile his ego really was. Could he take criticism? "You've got the power, but your release is late."

He nodded. "Yeah, it felt wrong." Then he frowned. "But a late release wouldn't put it in the gutter. Not if my aim was right."

Not only could he take criticism, but he could use it constructively. She admired a man who tackled problems analytically. "Yeah. Your aim was off, too. It's in the angle of your hips."

"I don't follow."

She hesitated then picked up a bowling ball. "Want me to show you?" Here was the test. A fragile ego would balk. An overinflated ego would claim he could figure it out on his own. A just-right ego would take the help.

"Can you walk me through it once?" he asked as he took the ball from her hands. "And then I'll try again on my own."

She grinned. Okay. So he had a just-right ego spiced with a dollop of confidence. She liked that.

"Let's do it without the ball first, okay?"

He nodded, practically dropping it in his haste. She laughed at the sight, but he simply shrugged. "I always obey promptly when a beautiful woman offers to teach me."

"I'll remember that," she said with a grin. Then she put her hands on his hips and guided him into the lane. She helped position him and then walked him slowly through the motion of rolling the ball. He listened attentively, following her physical cues with surprising speed. If his vision were normal, he'd probably be quite the athlete.

"Got it?" she asked.

"Got it." Then he flashed her a grin. "Unless you want to spend more time touching me. We don't even have to do it on the bowling lane. We could go—"

"Go get your bowling ball, Sam," she drawled.

"Right." He did. Then he positioned himself exactly as she'd suggested. He moved through the motions, bent almost smoothly, released too early this time and...

"Ouch," he said. "Another gutter."

"Yeah. But you'll get it next time."

"Maybe I need more hands-on guidance." He crossed back to her side.

"Maybe you need to practice a bit. And try to relax. You're all stiff."

He waggled his eyebrows at her. "Always am around you."

"Ha ha," she said as she pushed him down off the lane. "Go sit down. It's my turn."

He moved, but she heard his response loud and clear. "Just 'cause it's a lame joke doesn't mean it's not true."

She didn't answer. Her face had heated in a blush and she had to sneak a peek at his groin. Was it true? He certainly kept her burners going just by the way he looked in his dark jeans and nice polo. Unfortunately, he was already sitting down, so she couldn't tell. Which meant she had to return her mind to the task at hand. Taking a breath, she moved smoothly through the motions, released the ball and...strike!

Hmmm. How would his ego handle her success?

"Hey!" he cried looking up at the monitors above the lane. "A strike!"

"Yup."

"Cool! Should I cry mercy now? Or do you need to trounce me completely?"

"Trounce."

"Very well," he said with a dramatic sigh. "But only because you promised me a reward."

"And it'll be a good one," she said as she handed him his ball. She hadn't even had to act modest. How often did that happen?

He didn't gutter again. No strikes, but he managed a couple spares. He seemed very focused whenever he picked up the ball. That told her he took whatever task he performed seriously. He asked for more pointers, and she had to adjust his stroke a couple more times. He listened closely and really tried to implement what she said, which was a miracle all on its own.

And then, the moment he released the ball, he became another person. He laughed, he teased and he made off-color jokes. When a little girl came toddling into their lane, he was more than charming with her. And when the kid's mom came over, complete with triple-D breasts, he was polite there as well, just not overly charming. No ogling and no strain. Good date material all around.

He even agreed to another game, assuming, of course, that she doubled her reward. Since she'd decided that his reward would be a night in her bed, she had no problem doubling it. Nothing she'd seen so far had her doubting that he was the perfect fling.

Except, of course, the way he'd talked with the little girl. The child was five-and-a-half years old, on the verge of tears, and confused in the big bowling alley.

Sam had sat down on the floor so that he could be eye level with her. He didn't talk down to the kid, but listened patiently to what she had to say, which was a string of endless babbling about a doll and ugly shoes. Then he managed to charm the girl's full name out of her. They hadn't needed the information since the mom came dashing up, but the damage was done. Julie had seen him as more than just a fantasy. She had seen that he would make a great father someday.

And that, of course, made him the opposite of the perfect last-minute fling before returning to Nebraska. And that had thrown off her score for the last part of her game because a part of her was obsessed with deciding exactly what she wanted to do with Sam, her Elevator Man.

"So? So?" Sam pressed as the last frame was scored. "Did I make my goal?"

Julie laughed. "That all depends. What was your goal?"

"Two goals," he said as he peered at the screens above the lane. "First was to double my score."

"Too easy!" she cried. "Your first score was forty-two."

"Baby steps," he said primly.

"Well, you succeeded. A hundred and eight."

"Yes!" He struck a macho pose that made her laugh. "And your second goal?"

He sobered slightly, and stepped closer to her. She didn't know what he intended, but she went eagerly into his arms when he tugged her tight. "Did you have fun?" he asked. "Did I ruin it for you?"

She pulled his face around to hers, then decided to go for the full PDA. She kissed him on the mouth, slowly, sweetly and—eventually—with tongue. "I had a great time," she said a while later. "I think I needed to get out almost as much as you."

She felt his shoulders ease as even more tension flowed out of his body. "I'm glad you insisted," he said into her ear. "I forget sometimes that little challenges are just as powerful as the big ones. Forget global marketing and corporate restructuring. There was just as much joy—and a whole lot of immediate satisfaction—with *not* bowling a gutter ball."

She smiled at him, but as she pulled back from him, her thoughts were confused. "Global marketing? Corporate restructuring? This is part of your daily life?"

She felt him tense all the way from the tip of his red ears to his knees. "Uh, um, yeah."

"Oh, right! Probably with Mr. Finn."

Sam blinked as if startled she'd figured it out so easily. "Julie—"

"Let me guess. You two geeks pretend it's Monopoly or something, only more real world." At his confused look, she explained. "My brother, the one in the navy, he used to be a big gamer. He and his friends would spend hours discussing global domination if he had an army plus X-ray vision or something."

Sam raised his eyebrows. "Sounds like I'd really like your brother."

"Takes a geek to like a geek, though don't say that too loud around his navy pals."

"Promise. Mum's the word on global domination." Then he dropped his head onto the top of hers. "So I believe you owe me a reward."

"I do at that," she answered. Then she twined her fingers into his. "But first, I thought we could take a walk. Some place less noisy. If you—"

"Yes. Yes, yes, yes, yes. Right now, please."

She laughed. Clearly, he'd had his limit of real-world bowling. Just as well. She was extremely interested in spending more time talking with him, in figuring out what was the Sam story. She knew in her heart, it was a bad choice on her part. She really shouldn't want to know more about her fantasy lover.

But she wanted to know Sam. She wanted to explore his thoughts and his history. She wanted to just be with him. Which was exactly the opposite of her Elevator Man fantasy, but what the hell. Tonight was a night for breaking past comfort zones. Perhaps it was her turn now. Perhaps it was time to forget Elevator Man and just talk to Sam.

"I live nearby," she said. "There are a ton of great little shops and stuff. It's a good night for a walk."

"Great idea," he said. "You lead."

"Not a problem," she answered, even though she wasn't sure exactly where this was leading.

Ten minutes later they were climbing into her car. Because of his vision problems, Sam didn't own a vehicle. Between taxis and public transportation, he got along just fine, he said. So she'd driven them to the bowling lanes. She heard him sigh in relief the moment the car doors shut and they were inside a quiet, dark interior.

"That was tougher than you expected, huh?" she asked in sympathy.

"Yes. But like I said earlier, it was good for me. Thank you."

"Next date, you pick what we do." She said the words casually, but inside, she realized she'd crossed an internal barrier. She hadn't wanted to make plans with her fantasy man, but here she was practically begging him to take her out.

"Deal," he said too quickly for her to change her

mind. "Um, how about tomorrow night? After your meeting at RFE."

"Sure," she answered, though she was confused by the sudden tension in him at the offer. "I can call you right after I'm done. What's your cell—"

"Just hit the number for maintenance. I'll be, uh, I'll be right there waiting."

"But what if the meeting goes late?"

"Trust me," he said. "I'll be right there."

She had started backing out of her parking space, so she couldn't look at him, couldn't study his face for clues. Something was making him nervous, tightening his voice and clipping his words, but she hadn't a clue what.

"So what should we do tomorrow?" she asked to fill the increasingly uncomfortable silence.

"Let's leave that for tomorrow. That'll give me a chance to think up something great."

She shot him a look. "No staying in the building. We gotta get out."

He shook his head. "No promises. Tomorrow night is my night."

"Okay, okay. I suppose I can't complain about the other entertainments you planned for me."

"And don't you forget it!" he said with mock severity. "Though, I'm not sure I can top what we've already done."

She reached out and touched his hand. "You don't have to top it," she said sweetly. "Just top me. And bottom me. And everything else in the middle me." Then she laughed as he groaned.

"Damn, woman! We're in a moving car! You can't say something like that to a man and *not* let him follow up!"

"My night," she said primly. "And we're going for a walk."

"Yeah. Straight into your bedroom."

"Nope. Down by the lake."

"You're a cruel, cruel woman." His sigh was loud, dramatic and clearly heartfelt, causing her to laugh again.

"I already know we have chemistry, Mr. Elevator Man. Now I want to know if there's more."

He sobered and his hand shifted until his large fingers engulfed hers. "Is that what this is? Are we taking our relationship to a higher level?"

She shrugged. "Why not? Just so long as you understand—"

"Three weeks. Yeah, I remember."

"I was going to say that you still have to fulfill your Elevator Man duties," she lied. She *had* actually meant to remind them both about her three-week deadline. "I do expect hot fantasy sex tonight, you know."

"Oh, my God, the pressure!" he said in mock horror. "But I don't have any of my gizmos with me!"

"Don't worry," she said, her blood already heating as much from their laughter as from the sexual innuendo. "I'm sure the equipment you have with you will be more than adequate."

"Only because you have always provided excellent inspiration."

She was grinning as they hit Lake Shore Drive. However, when she finally made it to her apartment, she steered him out of the garage and straight onto the street. He complained, but only in a teasing tone. They both knew that the minute he got her indoors in private, nothing would stop them from stripping naked and doing whatever came to mind. And she had a *lot* in mind.

So they walked along the pathways, idly discussing the art in gallery windows or jewelry for sale by street vendors. They chatted about weather and family, about movies and high school. They even argued politics without so much as a ruffle. Thanks to his family situation, he was extremely aware of laws that affected the handicapped, and he wasn't shy about expressing his views. And whereas she knew very little about those issues, she was extremely aware of the cost of education and how funds directed to the handicapped had to come from somewhere, often the educational budget. Her high school was case in point regarding how very sparse a public education could be.

By the time they made it back to her apartment, it was well after dark. It didn't matter. She couldn't get enough of him. He seemed to feel the same. A moment later, he was stripping her out of her clothes. She was naked and his mouth was on her breast when her phone rang.

She ignored it, and both of them murmured impatient curses as the ring tone kept going. Eventually—thankfully—it ended. Then there was another chime to notify her of a voice message before it finally went silent. Which allowed her to get back to making sure Sam was fully naked. His jeans were just open, not off, and she wanted to feel his bare legs tangled with hers.

"Where's the bedroom?" Sam asked against her belly.

"Just beyond the couch. Right corner," she answered.

He frowned and lifted his head. She reached up and

flicked on a lamp revealing her efficiency apartment in all its plain glory.

"No money, remember?" she said as he took in the tiny space. She had one large room that included a kitchenette. They were stretched out on the couch right now, which was the centerpiece of the room. To the left was a card table and folding chair, to the right her futon bed. "But at least I've got a real bathroom," she said as she gestured past their feet. "Complete with a clawfoot bathtub."

"Let me guess, it's got plenty of space if you're a midget."

"Well, so long as you're a small midget." Then she pulled herself more upright on the couch, abruptly self-conscious about her lack of material wealth. "Do you have a problem with this?"

He shook his head slowly, his gaze traveling over every inch of her tiny space. "Actually I was thinking how homey this feels. Who did the artwork?"

"Karen. It was her housewarming gift to me."

"She's good." Then he looked down at her with a smile that made her toes curl. "But you're better."

"Why? Because I'm naked?" She put a bit of challenge in her voice to cover her embarrassment. She had carefully constructed the image of a successful businesswoman at work, but now he was seeing the real state of affairs. Now he knew how very poor she was and had been for a while.

"No," he answered. Then he flashed her a grin. "Well, yes, but also because I like the way your mind works."

She shifted. "I don't think we're talking about mind, here."

He laughed as he gestured around them. "Wanna

know what I see here? I see warm colors done in soft fabrics." He stroked a burnt orange corduroy pillow that her mother had made. It perfectly complemented the overstuffed brown velveteen couch they were lying on.

"There's no clutter here," he continued. "Books are in the bookcase, dishes on the rack."

"It's easy to be neat when you don't have anything."

"Oh, you have stuff. There's that stack of work over on your card table. I've seen your wardrobe, too. Good professional clothes, but with colors and creativity." He shifted back, giving her a good look at the sculpted expanse of his chest. But, oddly enough, it was his words that held her attention.

"My place is all cold metals, tools and gizmos. Hell, even my sheets are black. And there's clutter everywhere. But you…" His words faltered and she couldn't resist leaning forward to touch his arm.

"What? I'm a girl?"

He smiled. "You're creative *and* organized. That's a rare combination." His gaze came back to hers. "I'm sorry your business is struggling," he said. "But look around you. Someone who lives like this has both the passion and the discipline to make it. It'll just take time. Or a really good break."

She blinked, startled to realize that her eyes were tearing. He couldn't know what his words meant to her, that someone else believed in her, just from seeing her apartment.

"Oh, hell," he cursed as he saw her face. "I didn't mean to make you cry."

"No, no!" she gasped as she grabbed a tissue and wiped her face. And how ridiculous was this? She was sitting on her couch naked and sobbing because he'd

paid her a compliment. "You don't understand." She
blew her nose, then took a deep breath. "This was such
a huge step for me and Karen, setting up Web Wit and
Wonder two years ago. I would never have done it,
but we had the money saved up and a big contract to
boot."

He nodded. "The organic foods thing."

"Yeah," she said as she threw out her tissue. "How'd
you know about Happy Farm?"

"It's on your website."

"So it is," she said softly, warmed even more that he
had taken the time to read the company bio. "I had it
all worked out. It was enough to cover office rent and
expenses for a year. I thought that would be enough time
to find more work, to make a go of it in Chicago."

He shifted on the couch. They were still naked, but
there was nothing sexual in his touch as he tucked her
tight into her arms. "It was a good idea. You had to take
the jump. If you didn't risk it then, you'd never have gone
anywhere."

"That's what I thought!" she said as she dropped
her head back against his chest. "Then Happy Farms
decided to go with a bigger advertising firm—"

"Jerks!"

"And the economy shifted. We've had jobs along the
way, but—"

"Nothing big enough to cover your rent, much less
your other expenses. It's not your fault. You work harder
than anyone I know. You just didn't get the break you
needed."

She nodded. He understood. And his quiet confidence in her abilities bolstered her flagging self-esteem.
"I tried so hard," she said, burying her face against
his body.

"You'll make it," he said quietly. "It's just a matter of time." Then he pressed a kiss to her forehead. "Julie, what if you could stay in your office suite rent-free?"

She released a single bark of laughter. "What? You think the landlord would trade sexual favors for rent?"

He choked on that, and she had to wait a moment while he coughed his windpipe clear. "Um, no. You may not realize it, but the guy who owns the office building also owns RFE."

She stilled, then slowly shifted so she could look at his face. "The same guy I'm meeting with tomorrow?"

He nodded, his expression sober. "Without having to cover rent, you could probably—"

"Hang on for another year, maybe. There's no lack of penny-ante jobs. I just let them slide to concentrate on the bigger ones. I needed to land a big contract in order to keep the office."

He nodded. He obviously understood the basics of business accounting. "So if you had free rent, would you stay?"

She bit her lip, the fantasy spinning out in her head. By staying where she was, she could keep up the appearance of a successful company. She could take as many little jobs as she could scoop up while she kept searching for a bigger contract. She wouldn't have to leave Chicago, wouldn't have to go home in ignominious defeat and try to start her life over again. So many things would line up for her if she didn't have to pay rent.

She let her head drop back onto his arm, her eyes closing as she took her time and really relished the fantasy. "Mmm, Sam. Wow, that's a pretty dream."

She felt him stiffen at her words. "A dream?"

She opened her eyes. "Yeah, a dream. You didn't think I'd really take you up on it, did you?"

"Er..." he began, but stopped when she laughed.

"Sam, I doubt Mr. Billionaire Finn got that wealthy by allowing people to hang out in his building rent-free."

"He's not really a billionaire. That's just the press."

"All the more reason for him to demand rent. And it doesn't matter." She abruptly shifted, straightening up to look in him the eye. To his credit, his gaze bobbed only the tiniest bit as her breasts bounced in front of him. "I'm not going to let you trade on your friendship with Mr. Finn just to get me lowered rent."

He shifted. "Why not? I could do it, I'm sure. If not rent-free, at least cheaper rent."

She shook her head, awed by what he was offering to do for her. Not many people would risk their friendship to a millionaire just to keep her around. "You're sweet, Sam. You're more than sweet. You've made me feel so much better about..." She took a deep breath and forced the words out. "About failing out here in Chicago."

"You haven't failed," he said firmly. "You just need more time."

She shrugged, the motion feeling easier with every breath. "But I haven't got any more time. Or any more money."

"But you could," he pressed. "I have money. What if I gave you a loan?"

"Oh, God, you are perfect, aren't you?" she said, overwhelmed by a wave of total adoration.

"Why do I get the feeling that you're going to say no to that, too?" He spoke drily, but his caress on her arm was beyond tender.

She pressed a kiss to his lips. "Thank you, Sam. Thank you for making me feel better about leaving."

He took hold of her shoulders, gripping her firmly. "I was trying to get you to *stay*."

"And what you did was make me feel like I'm not a failure. That I am strong enough to rise to fight again."

"Well, of course you are—"

"So thank you, Sam. And no thank you on the loan."

"But Julie," he pressed, "what if I could do it? What if I could get you lowered rent?"

"You can't—"

"But what if—"

"Sam!"

Ring. Her cell phone again. Julie frowned and looked at the time. Who would keep calling her at this hour? Only her family. And only if there were an emergency.

She scrambled off Sam's lap and dove for her purse. She didn't get to it in time. It was buried in her bag. But she hauled it out enough to read who had called.

"I've missed twelve phone calls," she said, alarm tightening in her gut. "All from home."

She thumbed the callback button, her gaze immediately going to Sam's as she pressed the phone to her ear. He stood up silently, coming to her and wrapping her in his arms, his body large and comforting as they both waited for someone to answer.

11

SAM FELT HER BODY TENSE, her shoulder actually vibrating with anxiety. They were both naked. Five minutes ago, they'd had something very different on their minds. But now, Julie held her phone to her ear and clearly found it difficult to breathe.

There was nothing he could do but stand around and wait. And pray. So he pressed a kiss to Julie's shoulder, then grabbed a throw blanket off the couch to wrap around her. She flashed him a grateful smile.

"Mom?" he heard her gasp. "Mom, what's going on? Is everything all right?"

Sam waited along with her, his breath held, his hands ready for anything. Whatever she needed. And then Julie sagged in complete relief.

"Oh! Oh. Um, yeah. I was, I was going to tell you soon."

Sam released his breath. Okay, no traumatic situation at home.

Julie covered her phone to explain to him. "Mom called Karen about my birthday and found out about, you know, the business. When she couldn't reach me on my phone earlier, she got worried."

Sam nodded as she returned to her phone call.

"No, Mom. I was, well, I went out bowling. I figured I had to practice. You know, for when I come home."

Her voice was steadying, her body shifting into a more relaxed stance. Reluctantly, Sam took his cue from her. He stepped away and grabbed his pants, pulling on the denim with swift movements. Then he reached for his polo, but connected with Julie's hand instead.

She was still talking with her mother. Outlining exactly what had happened with her company. He knew he shouldn't be listening, but couldn't stop himself. She'd overextended. It wasn't uncommon in small companies. His own would probably have folded at that stage, too, but he'd been in a different economy and a vastly different field.

"It's okay," he mouthed.

"Just a minute, Mom."

"We can talk tomorrow," he said once she'd covered the phone again.

"No!" She twined her fingers in his and tugged him close. "This won't take long. Really. Just…can you stay?"

Of course he could stay. He was just trying to be respectful of her privacy. But he wanted nothing more than to spend time with her. All night long with Julie? He would sit through hours of a parental phone call for that.

"Sure," he said. At her direction, he settled down on the couch. A moment later, she curled up next to him. He enfolded her in his arms as she continued to talk into the phone.

"It sucks, Mom, but I'm okay. I, um…" She glanced

back at Sam and flashed him a smile. "I'm starting to feel better about it now. Really. And I swear I'll pay you back—"

Silence.

"Thanks, Mom." Her voice broke as she struggled against tears. Sam tightened his hold on her and she automatically tucked closer into his chest.

"I know," she said in a quiet voice. "I'm just, well, I'm packing things up. I need to regroup. Figure things out."

More silence as she listened to her mother. Sam found himself waiting for any clue from her. He heard the hitch in her breath and felt his chest grow wet. She was crying even as her voice remained upbeat.

"Yeah, I know."

He stroked her back, and he wished… He wanted… Well, he just wanted. He wanted things to go better for her. He wanted her to be happy. And he wanted to be with her when things did turn around. And he wanted it all with a need that burned through his gut.

But she wasn't going to take his money. She wasn't going to change her plans. She was going back to her family who obviously loved her. Back to Nebraska where she would lick her wounds and think up a new plan for her life. And she would do it all without him.

"Thanks, Mom," she said. "I gotta go now, but I'll call tomorrow. Actually," she added, her voice brightening, "I have a meeting with a big company tomorrow. It probably won't go anywhere, but maybe…"

Sam winced as another knife cut through his gut. Tomorrow's meeting had little to do with saving her business and more about confessing his lies to her. A talk with Ginny today had confirmed his fears. The last thing RFE needed was a small marketing firm, especially since they were already contracted with a big one.

"Love you, Mom! G'night!"

She clicked her phone shut and he released his hold on her so that she could drop it on the TV tray beside the couch. His plan was to kiss her gently and let her tell him good-night. That was, after all, exactly what he did when he was hurting. The last thing he wanted was anyone around him.

But he never got the chance. As soon as the phone left her fingers, she choked on a sob. And then, abruptly, she buried herself in his chest and started crying for real. Big gasping sobs, her body shaking with her emotions. She never spoke. She didn't have the breath. She just sobbed while he held her tight and wished for a miracle.

He wanted to say something to her, but he didn't have the words. At least none that would help when your business, your entire life for the last few years, was crumpling around you. He wanted to kiss her, to distract her from her pain, but he knew that's what they'd been doing the past few days. And mind-blowing sex only went so far. All he could do was hold her as she cried.

"It's okay," he murmured. "It'll be okay. We'll find a way." Ridiculous words, but all he had. "It'll be okay."

Eventually her sobs eased. She went from gasping to stuttered hiccups to shuddering breaths. And then, she exhaled a long, slow sigh. He stopped speaking. He wasn't saying anything anyway. Finally, he felt her body slowly unclench.

"God," she rasped. "I'm sorry."

"No. It's fine." Then he pressed a kiss into her hair. "You probably needed to let that out."

"I guess," she said as she pulled back. He didn't want to let her go, but he forced his hands to open. "But I didn't need to let it out all over your chest."

She reached for a tissue to blow her nose. Then she took another and wiped off his chest. His belly quivered at her stroke, and he flushed as he took over the clean-up. The last thing she needed was for him to get all horny right now. Problem was, she was a turn-on for him no matter what she was doing.

"Thank you, Sam," she said, her eyes huge and watery. "I don't think I could have told them without you here."

He touched her cheek. "Yes, you could have. You're stronger than you think."

Her lips pulled back into a trembling smile. "Maybe. But being with you makes me feel like less of a failure."

He frowned at her and changed to his CEO voice, one that never failed to get everyone's attention. "You didn't fail, Julie. You just ran out of time. That's not failure."

"Tell that to my business loans," she said with a grimace.

Clearly, she was immune to his CEO voice. So he decided to speak from the heart. "You're the furthest thing from a failure I've ever known. You're hurting right now. That's normal. But you're already looking for your next plan, your next step. You'll find it. I know you will."

She sighed and pressed her fingers to his lips. A simple press that became a soft stroke. "What if I'm not cut out for the big city? Chicago's a tough town."

He pushed away her fingers. "You're a tough cookie."

"But what if—"

He put his own fingers over her mouth. "Don't what-if, Julie. You're good enough. You're smart enough—"

"But—"

"Don't argue with me!"

Her eyes widened in surprise, but her lips curved in appreciation. And thankfully, she didn't speak.

"You won't take my help or my money. Okay. Take some advice: give yourself some time to recover. Re-group, restructure, refinance. Whatever. But don't ever doubt yourself. Question your methods, your plan, but never, ever question yourself. You *are* good enough."

She stared at him, tears welling in her eyes. Hell, he'd made her cry again. But she wasn't arguing with him. And when she slowly pulled his hand away from her face, she was smiling.

"Is that how you talk to Mr. Finn?"

He frowned, unsure how to answer. "Uh, no. He rarely has a crisis of confidence. Though, uh, lately, he's been struggling a bit more."

"Good thing he has you to point the way."

He looked at her, completely at sea. It was really hard for him to think of himself in the third person. Better to bring the focus back on her. "I just call 'em how I see 'em."

"Really?" she drawled. There was a hint of playfulness entering her expression. "Would you like to know what I see?"

"Uh, sure?"

"I see a man who better kiss me quick or I'm going to jump him."

He arched his brows. His lower region did a hell of a lot more than that. "And that would be a bad thing?"

"I might rip his clothing. I might tie him to my bed-post and never let him leave."

His gaze flickered to the corner. "You have a fu-ton."

"I have your handcuffs."

He started. "Really?"

"Really." Then she stood up, stepping backward just enough to let the blanket slip slowly down her body. A moment later, she was standing before him all pris-tine and beautiful and completely naked. Her skin was flushed, her nipples were tight and her eyes gave him an invitation that made all of his blood desert his brain.

Without even thinking about it, he stood up and started stalking toward her. "Better get those cuffs now," he said in a low, dangerous voice.

Her brows arched. "Oh? Why?"

"Because if you don't chain me down now, I'm going to overpower you." He extended his hand and cupped her breast. She shivered at his touch, but didn't back away. Not until he pinched her nipple. Then she jumped backward with a gasp. "I'm going to throw you down on your futon and do incredible things to both of us."

"Think you can catch me?" she taunted, as she backed away.

"Oh, yeah." And just like that he lunged. He caught her around the waist and flipped her over his shoulder. She squealed and nearly squirmed out of his grip, but he was strong and she wasn't fighting nearly as hard as she pretended.

He kneeled at the edge of her futon and half flipped, half rolled her down. Then he followed, pinning her easily with his weight.

"Now what, big boy?" she taunted. "Your jeans are on."

True enough. Thankfully, he had big hands. He cuffed her wrists above her head with his left while his right flowed down over her body. Shaping one breast, he lifted the nipple enough that he could nip it with his teeth. She was arching beneath him before he could even think about teasing the other side.

"God, yes, Sam! Don't stop!"

He had no intention of stopping. But he had lied about overpowering her. She didn't need the alpha-man treatment tonight. She just needed a thorough loving. So he took his time. He teased every inch of her body until she was quivering from erotic need. Every part of her got special attention. He even delved his hands into her hair and massaged her scalp.

She was sobbing with need by the time he finally stripped off his jeans. She was the one who tore open the condom packet and rolled the latex down over him. And then she pulled him down on top of her, tugging his ear close so she could whisper into it.

"Take me to the top, Elevator Man."

"Yes, ma'am," he answered as he thrust into her. He slammed as deep as he could go, and yet it wasn't enough. Another slam, and she went over the edge, arching into him with a cry. But he couldn't stop, even with her gripping and convulsing around him.

He thrust again and again, needing to bury himself in her so deep that he was written in her bones. His orgasm was explosive. His body pumped into her, his mind, his very being. He was hers.

Far from etching his name into her consciousness, he discovered he'd just done the opposite. He'd forever tied himself to her. No matter if she left in three weeks or three thousand years. She could forget him tomorrow, dump him without so much as an email goodbye.

While he, on the other hand, would think of her, want her, *need* her forever.

The knowledge didn't sink in immediately. It came in the blinding flash of his orgasm, but it was during the afterglow that reality hit.

He loved her.

"What time should I set my alarm?" she asked groggily from where she was curled against his side.

"What?" He loved her.

"My alarm. Tomorrow. I don't want you to get in trouble at work."

"What?"

She shifted, lifting up slightly to look at him. "With your boss. What time do you have to be at work?"

He couldn't think. He couldn't process anything but the sure understanding that he loved her.

"Seven o'clock okay?" she said as she twisted around to set her alarm clock. "That'll give us plenty of time to both shower and grab a latte before nine. Unless you need to be there by eight?"

"Um, nine is fine." No wait, he realized. He had a nine-thirty meeting with one of the project committees, and he hadn't checked their specs yet. He groaned.

"Slave driver, huh?" she said as she settled back against his side.

"What?"

"Your boss. It's Mr. Nolten, right? Head of building security and stuff."

Right. She would assume that Sam the elevator maintenance guy worked for Nolten.

"He looks like a hard-ass to me," she continued.

"That's why I—that's why he was hired."

"Good choice for the building. Sucky choice for the working schlubs beneath him."

She stretched up, rolling her delicious body over his to drop a kiss on his lips. He clutched her tight in reaction, stretching into her kiss only to have her move away too fast.

"Don't worry," she continued, as she flipped over to snuggle backward against him. Then she reached over and grabbed his wrist, pulling him around her until they were spooned tight. God, she felt good.

"You've got sick days, right?" she finished, her voice dropping into a sleepy murmur.

"What? Um..." The boss didn't get sick days. He either worked or he didn't. And in this case, if he didn't show up for the meeting, then it would have to be rescheduled. The project wouldn't move forward until he okayed it, and that meant he'd be paying a team of engineers to stand around twiddling their thumbs while they waited for him.

"Just call in sick tomorrow. I'd skip out, too, but I want to beef up on RFE stuff before my meeting. See if I can come up with anything brilliant."

He groaned. "Don't work too hard on that."

"Ha! If I'm going for a Hail Mary meeting, then I damn well am going to do some beforehand research. And prayer."

He sighed. Lord, she was going to be so furious when she found out he was James S. Finn, not Sam the maintenance schlub. And that there really wasn't any legitimate work for her at RFE. It was just a lame attempt by him to keep the love of his life from leaving for Nebraska.

The love of his life.

Leaving for Nebraska.

He groaned, unwilling to process either statement. She couldn't possibly be the love of his life. And she wouldn't leave him for Nebraska. He had to find a way to keep her here.

"So are you calling in sick?" she asked. "Do I let you sleep tomorrow morning?"

"No," he said morosely. "I'll get up with you and face the day. Whatever comes."

Or leaves.

Back to Nebraska.

Hell. Talk about a Hail Mary.

<u>12</u>

JULIE SHIFTED HER SWEATER, adjusting the V-neck so that it revealed just enough cleavage to be attractive, but not so much as to be unprofessional. She was in her office suite, making last-minute touches before heading to the elevator and the top floor.

Everything she'd read about James Finn, CEO of RFE, said he was a recluse, locked in his lab inventing stuff while others handled the production, legal and marketing end. Such a guy, she had decided, would not appreciate the power suit approach, but a softer sweater and trouser pant look. She kept her makeup understated, but made sure her brief outline of possible marketing concepts was absolutely pristine. If by some miracle, he wanted something to hand to his marketing VP, then she had it ready.

Showtime, she thought as she headed out toward the elevator bank. There was something freeing in a last-ditch attempt to save her company. Logically, the entire meeting was ridiculous. Even if Mr. Finn loved everything she put together, no corporation moved fast enough to save her. And they certainly wouldn't *pay* fast enough to stave off her creditors. And yet, here she was, concepts in hand, ready to give it her all. If she was going to fail on this pitch, then she was going to fail with everything she had. Then she'd go back to Nebraska with her head held high, knowing she'd tried absolutely everything.

She stepped into the elevator, and her mind naturally went to Sam. But she couldn't think about him! She couldn't mentally relive every second of the intense encounter they'd shared here or she'd show up at RFE in a lust-filled haze. So she forced her mind down a different path.

She understood now why Sam and Finn were such close friends. What little she could gleam about the robotics inventor showed that both men came from a blue-collar family, had a fascination with electronics and had decided not to pursue a pedigreed education, despite their obvious intelligence. By all accounts, the CEO had a brilliant, innovative mind. He didn't seem to be hampered by his lack of formal education. In some ways, that might help him think outside of the box. Instead, he relied on his staff for the formal training—PhDs abounded in the company roster—while he led the company with a firm, but nonpublic hand.

And now she was going to meet him face-to-face. She'd scoured the internet for some picture of Mr. Finn, but could only turn up his lawyer's face. Roger Martell was clearly the public image of RFE, leaving Mr. Finn to work in his lab.

The elevator dinged, and she stepped out into the corporate lobby of RFE. It was airy, with a gleaming display of gadgets, and it was presided over by a very perky blonde receptionist. "Good afternoon, Miss

Thompson," the young woman greeted her in cheerful accents. "Mr. Finn will be with you shortly."

"Thank you," Julie responded and would have found a seat, but the receptionist was clearly bored and desperate for someone to talk to.

"Would you care for some refreshments while you wait? We have a variety of drinks and cookies." At those words, she pressed a button and a selection of sweets and bottled drinks slid out from the wall. "I just love that," she said as she pressed the button again. The tray slid away. Then another press and it appeared again.

"Um, no thanks. I'm fine."

"Let me know if you change your mind. My name's Claire, by the way." Then the first chords of Beethoven's Fifth sounded, startling Julie. There it was again. Dum dum da dum!

"That's Mr. Finn's chime now. Pompous, huh? I think Roger programmed it just to tweak the boss. They're best friends and do that kind of stuff to each other all the time."

So, RFE had a casual, tease-each-other climate. "Sounds like this might be a fun kind of place to work."

"Oh, it's great fun! Except when they set things on fire. Or when Mr. Finn gets gloomy and won't see anyone. Or gets inspired and locks everyone out of the lab. He doesn't really get gloomy often, but that last part— the inspired part—he does that a lot."

More good information. She stepped forward, ready to ask more questions, but a fairylike sparkle of sound shimmered through the air.

"Oh!" Claire stood up and pulled a stack of papers off the printer. "That's Roger's chime. And yes," she added in an undertone. "I think Mr. Finn programmed that." Then she waived to a set of closed metal doors on her left. "I've got to deliver these, but you can go on through the lab. Mr. Finn's in there."

Julie nodded and headed toward the doorway only to pause as a clear blue line began flashing on the floor right in front of it.

"Oh, right!" the receptionist said as she spun back to Julie. "I'm supposed to tell you that by crossing the blue line, you are waiving all right to sue us if something disastrous should happen to your items or your person. If you need to, there's a row of lockers to the left for your personal items. They're right next to the sign that details the agreement."

Julie was unsure what to make of that statement. "Is this more corporate teasing?"

The girl giggled. "Sounds that way, doesn't it? But no, it's serious. You won't be allowed to enter if you refuse to waive your rights."

"Isn't that rather limiting?" Julie asked. "How many people are so desperate to see Mr. Finn that they agree?"

Rather than answer, the receptionist gestured to a different door, one without the flashing blue line. "The waiver only applies to Mr. Finn's lab. You can see anyone else in the company without a disclaimer."

Julie nodded, understanding dawning. "So this is Mr. Finn's way of avoiding unwanted visitors?"

The woman nodded. "I was kinda surprised that he agreed to see you." Then she tilted her head, and Julie abruptly realized that Claire was much smarter than she first appeared. "So how do you know Mr. Finn?"

Julie had no intention of confessing that her connection to the reclusive Mr. Finn was through Sam. So rather than answer, she simply smiled and gestured at the blue line. "I waive my rights."

"Very well. And, if you should feel the need, alcoholic beverages are always available out here. As well as the cookies."

Julie glanced back and saw the mischievous smile on the woman's face. "This really does sound like a fun place to work," she said slowly.

"You have no idea," the receptionist drawled. Then she gave Julie a wave before disappearing though the normal door. Which left Julie a moment alone to smooth her sweater and dry her palms at the same time. Then she stepped across the blue line, feeling a little like Alice jumping into the rabbit hole.

The lighting was daunting, as if the entire lab was under spotlights, and she had to squint for a moment to allow her eyes to adjust. She had stepped into a hallway created by floor-to-ceiling metal shelves. She might have been tempted to touch the gadgets she saw there—everything from wheeled mini-cars to what looked like a slinky sprouting antenna—but the shelves were lined with a clear plastic that allowed her to see but not touch.

She stepped forward, entranced by the view, and the heels of her black pumps clicked as she hit concrete. Then stopped clicking as she stepped on something sticky. It was a pad set on the floor to remove debris from people's shoes. She'd seen something like them before outside of racquetball or squash courts.

She dutifully stepped a couple times on the pad, then moved slowly forward through a maze of tables with electronics, tools and who-knew-what else. Fortunately, the path was clear, though the sense of descending into the rabbit hole increased. Each twist and turn gave the impression of navigating a warren to the secret hearth of some beast. Especially since she heard no noise except for the whirl of electronic fans and the soft notes of classic Beatles music.

Finally, she rounded what had to be the last corner. There was a long L of a desk that was buried half under papers and a span of large monitors along the wall. The music, she now saw, came from a movie that was playing on one of the monitors, though no one appeared to be watching it.

To the left, she saw robotic clutter. That was the only thing she could call it as she peered at pieces of inventions that were clearly in process. And directly in front of her was a single stool on wheels—and no one in sight.

She bit her lip. Where was Mr. Finn? She could have called out, but that seemed rather presumptuous. Should she sit and wait?

Then she heard something to her left. A clatter of bolts on the concrete? A scrape of plastic? It was hard to tell. She turned toward it, even took a step in that direction. Then she squeaked in alarm as a tall figure popped up behind one of the tables.

He was tall, had dark curling hair and thick goggles on his face, but it was his coveralls that gave him away. It was Sam, her elevator man, holding what appeared to be a large metal spider on wheels which in turn seemed to be holding a dustpan filled with washers and a large brush.

"Sam!" she gasped. "You scared me!"

He looked at her, and his face colored all the way to his ears. But he also shifted into a smile that warmed her down to her toes. When had that started? she wondered. Sure, the sight of her personal elevator god could get her instantly horny, but never before had it warmed her deep inside. But then, after last night, she supposed it was natural that their relationship would be more… intimate? Personal? Close? She didn't know the right word. She only knew that the sight of him looking all flustered made her smile.

"Spill something?" she asked as she gestured to the dustpan filled with washers.

"Uh, kinda." He hefted the spiderlike robot. "Prototype of a domestic assistant."

She frowned, looking past the table to see the floor where he and the spider-thing had been. Washers, bolts and dust bunnies abounded. "Not the finished model, then?"

"Uh, no. Definitely not." He came forward, setting the robot back on the table behind him. "So, um, you look nice."

"Thanks! And it only took me a couple hours to throw it together," she quipped. Then she leaned forward. "I'm kinda nervous for this meeting. There's quite the mystique built up around Mr. Finn. Do you know where he is?"

"Mr. Finn isn't that scary. He, um, just has trouble with getting in over his head. Something starts and he doesn't know how to stop it. And it all gets out of control."

Julie shrugged. "Whatever his deal is, I'm supposed to be meeting with him. Should I just wait here?"

"Um, well, as to that…" Sam stepped around another table, accidentally knocking some widget over as he moved. His hands were fast as he grabbed it, but he took a lot of time replacing it where it belonged.

"What's the matter, Sam?" she said as she really looked at him. His hair stood up in all directions, his eyes behind his goggles were huge, and most telling of all, his hands which were normally so assured seemed to be fidgeting. "You seem really nervous."

"Well, yeah. Julie, I've got something difficult to confess…"

"Have you completely lost your freaking mind?" came a man's loud voice. He easily overpowered the movie's soundtrack as he maneuvered through the maze to reach the back. "Global initiative? Robotics for the third world? They can't even pay for gruel, much less what it would cost—"

Mr. Roger Martell rounded the corner, waving a stack of papers in his hand. She recognized him from all the publicity photos on their website. But at the sight of Julie standing there, the man clearly swallowed his words. His steps slowed and he frowned at her, his gaze narrowing as it hopped between her and Sam.

"Oh. Hello," he said as he looked curiously at her.

She smiled warmly. It wasn't Mr. Finn, but the CFO was definitely someone she wanted on her side. So she extended her hand in her best professional smile. "Hello. You're Roger Martell, aren't you? I recognize you from your website. I'm Julie Thompson of Web Wit and Wonder from downstairs. I've got an appointment with Mr. Finn, but I'm afraid he appears to be a bit late."

Mr. Martell's eyes narrowed even further as his gaze hopped to Sam. "I'm sorry?"

Julie glanced back at Sam who had a blush burning all the way up to his ears. Oh, hell, she suddenly thought. Was Sam *not* supposed to be up here? It would be just like him to come up here for moral support, provide the introduction, and then duck out. He was sweet that way. But obviously he hadn't counted on Mr. Finn being absent. Or that Mr. Martell would come in.

"I hope you don't mind," she said suddenly. "Sam here was just keeping me company until Mr. Finn arrives. We're old friends," she added, hoping that the lie would hold.

Mr. Martell shifted, his eyebrows climbing almost up to his immaculately tousled hair. "Old friends, you say?"

Julie winced. That's what she got for fudging the truth. "Well, it feels like that anyway. Sam's so sweet. Anyway, I have an appointment with Mr. Finn to discuss some marketing ideas."

Mr. Martell looked at her, then his eyes slid back to Sam. "Marketing ideas," he drawled, a gleam of mischief coming into his expression. "To pitch to Mr. Finn. While Sam, here, keeps you company."

"Yes," Julie confirmed. Clearly there was an undercurrent here she didn't understand. "Is there a problem—"

"Um, look," interrupted Sam as he stepped closer to her. "Julie, I've got to talk to you—"

"No, no," Julie countered before he could continue. Whatever he had to say to her could be handled later in private. Right now she needed to focus on Mr. Martell. Or Mr. Finn, if the man ever showed up. "You should go back to work, Sam. I don't want to get you in trouble with Mr. Nolten," she added, referring to Sam's boss, the head of maintenance and security.

"Oh, yes," drawled Mr. Martell. "Getting in trouble with Mr. Nolten would be bad."

"Stop it, Roger," Sam shot back, a curt edge to his voice.

Great, Julie thought. Now she was getting Sam in trouble with the CFO. "Do you know where Mr. Finn is?" she pressed, hoping to pull Mr. Martell's attention off of Sam. "We had an appointment."

"Right," he said, his expression shifting into a huge grin. "To pitch marketing ideas to Mr. Finn. But he's late and Sam here is keeping you company."

"Yes," she almost snapped. What the hell was going on? But before she could ask, Mr. Martell abruptly shifted to charming. He gave her a big smile before grabbing a lab rag and wiping off a stool for her.

"I'm so sorry," he said, all kindness. "Mr. Finn has been unavoidably detained."

"He has not—" said Sam.

"Oh, but he has," interrupted Mr. Martell. "In fact, he asked me to cover instead. I'd love to hear your ideas. But first, please tell me exactly how you and Sam know each other."

Before Julie could speak, Sam released a heavy sigh. "It's complicated."

"So I gathered," the CFO drawled.

"And it's private," inserted Julie firmly. She didn't like this man. She didn't like the way he was treating Sam, and really didn't like the undercurrents in his words that she didn't understand. But he was CFO of the company she was pitching. Any job with RFE would require his support. Sure, she would have preferred to meet with the mysterious Mr. Finn, but failing that, she would take what she could get. "Well, if you're covering, perhaps we should get started." She pulled out the press sheets on her company. "Web Wit and Wonder has developed an interesting approach to marketing on the web. These techniques cost relatively little and yet reap huge rewards. Now, Mr. Martell, you must understand that this was a blind meeting."

"Oh, please call me Roger."

She paused a moment, then nodded. "Very well, Roger. I'm not exactly sure what type of campaign Mr. Finn was looking for other than to increase his web presence. That is, after all, our speciality at Web Wit and Wonder. I put together some ideas based on the holes I see in your current market presence."

She leaned over and pulled out the pages she'd thankfully prepared this morning. She hadn't been sure that multicolored diagrams and market statistics were appropriate to the reclusive Mr. Finn. But for Mr. Martell, she was right on the button. He would want reports with all the trimmings.

"If you would take a look right here…" she began.

BLOODY HELL! Now what was he supposed to do? Sam hovered in the background of his own lab and cursed himself for being a damned chicken. He'd meant this meeting to be his confession. He'd gone over it and over it in his mind, but when Julie had walked in looking so soft and professional, he'd gotten tongue-tied. After last night's realization that he was in love, his need to come clean verged on massively urgent. But it had to be done right. The last thing he wanted was to lose her forever. He was just working himself up to the confession when Roger had walked in and blown everything to hell.

It hadn't taken long for his best friend to figure out the truth. Roger knew Sam hated the bimbos that dated him for his money. The bastard guessed he'd never told Julie who he really was. But what Sam hadn't expected was that Roger would take over the meeting. Obviously the jerk was checking Julie out. He was also torturing Sam in the process.

Meanwhile, Julie had launched into her pitch with real skill. Sam stepped forward, not hiding the fact that he was listening. Damn, his girl was good! Her concepts really were innovative, and he saw serious potential in them. She had identified holes in his current publicity strategy, gaps that his expensive advertising agency hadn't even considered.

One look at Roger's stunned face confirmed Sam's opinion. Yup, Julie was good. Her pitch was bang on. And given how little time she'd had to come up with her ideas, Sam was triply impressed.

"Here's what you've done on the web so far," she was saying as she walked Roger through her proposal.

Roger nodded as he scanned the page she'd given him. "Looks about right."

"It's all good, but is it really targeting the people you want? I thought RFE meant Robotics for Everyone."

"It does," Roger murmured, his keen gaze centered on the things she'd written.

"Then you need a grassroots campaign," she said. "To reach everyday people. Here's an outline of what we could do for you..."

Roger was shaking his head. "Everyday people can't afford what these robots cost. I have that argument with Mr. Finn every week." To his credit, Roger didn't even glance back at Sam, the Maintenance Man. Instead, he balled up a piece of paper and tossed it on Sam's desk. Sam had no doubt it was the very memo he'd written this morning about robotics for developing countries, and the very reason Roger had come storming in with the "Are you out of your mind?" rant.

"Well, I don't really know anything about your costs. But I would think that some of your products..." Julie reached into her briefcase and pulled out images from his company's website. "Is there a stripped-down version of this, for example?"

Sam peered over her shoulder. "Not yet. But there could be."

Julie glanced over at him, clearly surprised that he was still here. Well, of course, because a maintenance man would have no reason to be at a high-level marketing pitch. Didn't matter. No way was he leaving her alone with his smooth-talking, better-looking best friend.

Julie looked back at Roger. "Maybe that should be my next step," she said. "I need to find out exactly what products you're trying to market via the internet."

"That was the initial plan for the meeting," Sam inserted. Well, it was sort of the initial plan.

Roger arched a brow at Sam, his expression thoughtful. "Was it really?" Obviously the question had a double meaning. His friend was asking him what exactly had he intended. Sam squirmed. He'd meant this meeting to force himself to confess the truth. But instead, things had gone all backward and now he was deeper into his lies than ever before.

"Julie," he said, forcing himself to man-up. "I really need to talk to you."

"Of course—" she began, but then Roger interrupted.

"Yes, indeed," he said as he extended his hand to Julie. "Miss Thompson—it is Miss, isn't it?"

Julie straightened off her stool, obviously startled by the abrupt transition. But that was Roger—quick brain, quick decisions, and a pace that most people could only marvel at. "Um, yes. But call me Julie."

"I think I'll stay with Miss Thompson for now," Roger said as he flashed Sam a wry look. "Wouldn't want to be overly familiar with my boss's...er...meeting."

"Ha!" Sam snapped back.

"I'm sorry," began Julie, but Roger rolled right over her.

"Never mind. Inside joke. Very rude of me." Roger picked up her proposal and tapped the top page. "I find your ideas very compelling. But you should know that RFE already has a contract with a large advertising firm. Still, you're very smart. And very beautiful," he added with a wink. "I can see why Sam likes you."

Julie glanced back at Sam, but was kept from speaking as Roger barreled on.

"I'm pretty sure that our fearless leader isn't going to be showing up tonight for your meeting. He does that sometimes, you know, just flakes out at the oddest times. But we forgive him because he really does mean well."

Sam released his breath on a huff. He wasn't sure if his friend was trying to help or not, but it didn't matter. This had to end. "Julie, you have to understand that most of Mr. Finn's bio was created by marketing. Even his name isn't the name he usually goes by."

"Oh, look at the time," Roger called as he faked looking at his watch. "Miss Thompson, please stay awhile. Have Sam here show you the lab and a little bit of what RFE has been trying to do." He paused, his eyes warm as he shot a look at Sam. "There's no doubt that our leader is weird. He is a genius after all. But he's got a heart of gold. I hope you take that into consideration."

Julie frowned, clearly not following Roger's underlying message. "Well, of course," she said, but Roger was already waving goodbye.

"I'll have Claire order you something nice to eat up here. Oysters or strawberries dipped in dark chocolate," he said, listing well-known aphrodisiacs.

"That's not necessary," Sam began but Roger cut him off.

"My treat!" he called. "But you're going to have to pay me back for the wine!" And with that, he was gone. Which left Sam and Julie staring at each other in confusion, the same question still hanging over Sam's head.

What now?

13

JULIE WAITED UNTIL SHE thought she heard the doors whoosh shut behind Roger. Then she turned to Sam, searching his face for clues to how she'd done. His face was completely blank, except for a hint of panic that seemed to be lurking in his eyes.

"So, um, he's quite the character, huh?"

Sam blinked, then glanced at where Roger had disappeared. "You don't think he's, uh, sinfully handsome or anything?"

"Him? Well, yes, I suppose he is. I'll bet *he* certainly thinks so."

Sam shrugged. "Most women think so, too."

"Yeah, well I'm not most women." She flashed him her best minx smile. "I'm a coverall kind of gal."

"And thank God for that," he drawled. But the panic didn't leave his eyes.

"Are you afraid he's going to say something to Mr. Nolten?" She took a step forward, but didn't dare touch him. Not until she understood his mood better. "Roger seemed okay with you being here."

Sam flushed and shook his head. "No, it was fine that I was here."

"Then why…" Her thoughts finally linked together and a horrible suspicion filtered in to her mind. And the more she thought about it, the more likely it seemed. "Oh, God, you know something."

"What?"

"You know something about this job." She slumped back into her seat. "Was the pitch all wrong? I thought I did rather well, but—"

"No, no!" He rushed forward, but stopped short of arm's reach. "No, I thought you did great. Better than great." He jerked his chin back toward where Roger had disappeared. "He was impressed."

"Really?"

Sam nodded. "Really impressed."

She flushed, her mind scrambling a mile a minute. "You're just saying that because you're—" She cut off her words. She was about to say because he was her boyfriend. But he wasn't really her boyfriend, was he? There had been no commitment from either of them. They were more like, well, office buddies. With perks.

His gaze had zeroed into her face. "Because what?" he asked.

"Because you're my Elevator Man," she said, even though she knew the words were beyond lame. "It's, you know, part of the office sex code. You have to lie when your partner screws up."

He seemed to deflate before her eyes. "*You* didn't screw up," he said softly.

She frowned at his emphasis on the word *you*. Just exactly who did he think had screwed up? "Oh!" she said, a lightbulb going on in her brain. "You're upset because Mr. Finn didn't show." She leaped up, her relief palpable. "But don't you see, this was even better!"

Sam frowned. "Better? How?"

"Well, sure it would have been nice to meet Mr. Finn, but from everything I learned, Finn doesn't handle much of the marketing stuff."

"He doesn't."

"Right. So I have to impress Roger and the head of marketing."

"Ginny."

"Right. Well, wham, I just got a meeting with half of the two key people. Better, he encouraged you to tell me all about their products *and* he's buying us dinner. I'd say I more than impressed. I rocked!"

She danced over to him, letting herself feel the moment. Sure, things hadn't happened the way she'd planned, but they'd worked out. They'd worked out great!

"Unless," she drawled, "you don't think I did—"

"Stop fishing for compliments!" he said in a teasing tone. "You were spectacular."

"It's why I came to Chicago, you know. I could never work on a robotics campaign in Nebraska." She took a deep breath, letting the air fill her lungs. "I know this is a last-ditch effort. I know that it's still quite a long shot, but Sam, it's been really, really good for me." She abruptly leaned forward and pressed a hot kiss to his lips. "Between working on this campaign and your... um..."

"Expert distractions?" he offered, his expression wry.

"Let's call it perfect stress relief," she said with a grin. And then when he didn't respond, she softened her words to something closer to the truth. "And your wonderful friendship, too," she said.

He nodded, but his face didn't look any happier.

"Oh, don't be a sourpuss," she said, tweaking his nose flirtatiously. "I'm trying to thank you! This has been wonderful for me, whether Mr. Finn stiffed me or not."

Sam released a heavy sigh. "He didn't stiff you."

"Yeah," she said with a grimace. "I figure he's getting back at you, actually, for using your friendship to set up this meeting in the first place. You know, he arranges the meeting, then doesn't show. Perfect way to show that he won't let you backdoor people."

Sam slowly shook his head. "Julie, you're thinking way too hard about this. It's really something very simple. Maybe even funny actually—"

"I don't care what it is," she said, suddenly interrupting him. "I don't want to know. Whatever his deal is, it doesn't matter. Because Roger Martell, CFO, just told you to explain all about RFE's products. *And* he's paying for dinner. So you're not going to spoil this with talk of the bizarre Mr. Finn."

Sam rubbed a hand over his face. "Julie, if you would just listen a moment—"

"Really, Sam, I don't care!"

"But—"

"No!" She pulled him to his feet. He'd been slumping against Mr. Finn's desk, and she wasn't going to have any of his mysterious male moods right now. "You are supposed to tell me all about RFE's products."

"But—"

"I'm not going to hear anything out of you but that. And do you know why?"

He mutely shook his head.

"Because after you tell me everything I need to know to develop a kick-ass campaign, we're going to celebrate." And in case he didn't understand exactly how she meant to celebrate, she allowed her hand to flow down over his coveralls until she cupped his—

"Woah!" he cried, grabbing her wrist. But his eyes had gone darker, hungrier. "We are still at work, you know."

"And in Mr. Finn's secret lab!" she added as she shimmied against him. "Makes it more fun, don't you think? He could walk in on us at any moment."

"Uh, actually, he couldn't—"

"Shh!" she said as she leaned forward for a kiss. He clearly didn't intend to make it as hot as she did, but she persisted. She licked his lips. She nibbled around the edges. She pressed her entire body up against him.

He surrendered with a groan. Slanting his mouth over hers, he gripped her hips tight, and he angled it so that she was bending backward over Mr. Finn's desk. Talk about taking hot liberties!

When he finally pulled back enough to breathe, Julie used the moment to tug at his coverall zipper. "So, just how sure are you that Mr. Finn isn't coming back anytime soon?"

Sam abruptly leaned past her shoulder and tapped a few keys on the keyboard. Then she heard the sound of bolts being thrown throughout the room. "There. No one comes in now."

She frowned as she looked around. "There are dead bolts in the doors?"

"Not really. But that's the joy of computers," Sam said with a shrug. "They can generate just about any sound you want. But the meaning is the same. The lab is locked tight. You're trapped in here with me."

Really? she thought, her eyes scanning the rows and rows of gizmos. Just imagine what kind of trouble they could get into here. But that was too much work, and she was abruptly much too interested in the here and now. Sliding her heels up the back of his legs, she stretched herself backward across the desk.

"So," she offered with a slutty grin. "Wanna do me on the boss's desk?"

"Yeah," he said, in a no-nonsense tone. "I do."

"Well then—"

"But here's the deal. Tonight is your night. We're gonna do whatever you want."

She smiled. "Ooh. I like the sound of that."

"But tomorrow we have to talk. Honestly. No more excuses or delays."

She frowned. This sounded way more serious than she'd expected. "Sam—"

"No. You're going to have to listen to everything I have to say to you tomorrow. Everything. Okay?"

She shifted, and he helped her sit up on Mr. Finn's desk. Her blood was still simmering, but there were alarms going off in her brain. "How much is everything? I mean, what do you mean?"

He touched her face, stroking her chin tenderly, but his expression was stern. "I mean I haven't been completely honest with you."

She groaned. "You better not be married."

"I'm not!"

She released a huff of breath. "Sick? Gay? Alien pod person?"

"No, no, and what the hell?"

"Then—"

"I want more, Julie. I want to be more than just your office stress relief."

She smiled, her body practically wilting in relief. He wasn't married or sick. Those were the only things she was really worried about. "The rest are just details," she said as she went back to his zipper.

He caught her hand and held it still. "I'm a detail kind of guy."

She nodded. She knew he was. And more, she knew that despite the way they'd begun, he was not the kind of guy to bang women in the elevator. Last night had proved that to her. A late-night Lothario would have cut and run a dozen times last night. Certainly by the time she started sobbing all over him.

But he hadn't run. He'd stayed and made love to her as if she were the most precious thing on the planet. He was the staying kind. The forever kind. Except she was going back to Nebraska in just a couple of weeks.

"It's complicated," she hedged.

"I know," he answered. "Believe me, I know."

She was silent a moment as she tried to think rationally about their relationship. It couldn't work. She wasn't ready to commit to him, wasn't ready to promise to hang around in Chicago, buried in debt, so they could have hot monkey sex every night. The sex would be great, but she needed to take the next step with her life. And mostly, she needed to figure out what her next step would be.

"Okay," she finally said. "I swear. Hot sex tonight. Tomorrow, we talk. Honestly. Openly. Agreed?"

He lifted her hand and pressed a tender kiss into her palm. "Agreed."

Then he replaced her hand on his zipper. It was open halfway down his chest, right over his heart. She flattened her palm there, liking the feel of his heart thumping beneath her fingers, as he leaned in, nuzzling her neck just beneath her ear.

"Did you know that the lab is soundproofed?" he asked. "You can make all the noise you like. You can even scream."

"Really," she drawled as she abandoned his heart to slowly draw his zipper down. "What if you're the one who's screaming?"

She felt him grin against her neck. "Even better."

While she was busy tugging at his zipper, he slid his fingers underneath her shirt, popped the clasp on her bra and filled his large hands with her breasts. And wow, did that feel good...

"I love that you're so big," she murmured, as her head dropped back. "Your hands, your body, your—"

"This?" He ground against her. Jeans, coveralls and her trousers did nothing to blunt the hot force of him rubbing hard against her groin.

"Oh yeah," she said.

He whipped her sweater and bra off over her head. And when she emerged, he just leaned back and admired her, a grin on his face.

"You are the sexiest damn thing I've ever seen."

"Want me to talk dirty to you?"

His eyes widened in surprise. Then he nodded slowly.

"Should I tell you that all the time I was talking to Roger, I was thinking about you bending me over this desk?"

His mouth dropped open in shock, and she nearly laughed out loud at his reaction. "That's a lie," he rasped.

She shook her head. "No, it's not." Well, it wasn't a complete lie. He certainly had been a massive distraction throughout the whole meeting. "Now get naked, big boy, while I tell you what else I was imagining."

He immediately started shrugging out of his coveralls, his hands shaking so much he fumbled with the stiff fabric.

"While Roger was looking at my graphs, I was wondering exactly how many of these gizmos could be adapted into vibrators."

"You can stop mentioning Roger now."

"You're right," she said as she thumbed open the button of her trousers. He was going to flip when he saw the black lace thong she had on underneath. "I was actually thinking of being tied down on one of the worktables while you experimented on me."

Sam had his usual attire on underneath the coveralls: jeans and a soft tee. He didn't bother with the shirt but quickly shucked his jeans while she jumped off the desk. He didn't give her much room to maneuver, but she had enough to shimmy out of her trousers and give him a full look at her thong.

He popped out thick and hard and gloriously huge.

"I take it back," he said in a throaty growl. "*That* is the hottest thing I've ever seen."

She straightened up, wearing just the thong and her heels. Then she cupped her breasts and struck a pinup pose, butt arched high behind her. "Are you sure?" she asked. "Maybe we could find some other looks."

"Nope," he said, and she heard the rip of a foil packet. By the time she'd looked back at him, he was already rolling on the condom. "I had my own thoughts while you were mesmerizing Roger," he said.

"I thought we weren't going to mention—"

"And they involved you…" He grabbed hold of her hips. "On my desk…" In one motion, he stripped her thong past her knees. "At my mercy," he growled as he lifted her up and dropped her onto the surface of the desk.

"Oh, my," she cried, slipping into their earlier boss man/innocent secretary roles. "Am I to be punished again?"

He adjusted her hips, fitting himself straight to her center. She looked down, thinking that there was a sight she couldn't get enough of. Him, hot and huge for her. Her open and ready for him. Now she understood why erotic pictures were so popular.

Then he caught her chin, lifting her gaze up to his. "No pretend play, Julie. Not this time."

She arched a brow. "Okay—"

"Just you and me. Together." And then he rammed home.

She gasped, arching into the penetration. He filled her. He stretched her. And she wrapped her legs around him to grip him even tighter. They stayed like that for a moment. He was embedded deep inside her. She loved him there, held him close, and never wanted it to end.

"Kiss me," he whispered against her ear.

She shifted slightly, raising her hands to cup his cheek, to stroke his lips, to look into his eyes. She had not meant it to be anything more than a touch, a caress before the kiss. But once their gazes locked, it became something more.

This was Sam, she thought, open and vulnerable to her. In his dark eyes, she saw need. But she also saw tenderness, almost worship. Of her. She never thought she'd see a man look at her that way, all raw desire and fragile hope. It filled her vision. It consumed her thoughts. And a new emotion blossomed inside her. Wonder. Sheer awestruck wonder that this man would

look at her that way. That Sam could look at her like
that. The moment was so intense, that she lost all sense
of reality. She only saw him and the wondrous feeling
he created inside her.

He leaned forward slowly to kiss her. She met him
easily, passionately. Their mouths fused, their tongues
dueled, and lower down, their bodies began moving.
Still cupping his face with her hands, she tightened her
legs around him, lifting herself up. He helped her by
cupping her bottom, holding her at the perfect angle.

She arched, loving the slam of his groin against hers.
His hands were firm and steady. She never had any fear
that he would drop her. And still they kept kissing.

Then he twisted his face away, gasping for air as
he settled her back on the edge of the desk. One of his
hands slid around her hip to thrust a thumb between
them. She hardly needed it, but it didn't matter. He was
determined.

He stroked her once, hard, down and up. Then again.
By the third time, she was flying, pleasure roaring
through her. She heard him gasp something incoher-
ent as her muscles worked him. He stiffened against her
and released. With her legs wrapped around him, she
felt every contraction of his buttocks, every shudder as
it racked his frame.

And then he fell forward against her, his forehead
dropping to her shoulder. His breath was hot across her
skin as his body still contracted in uneven bursts that
sent tiny ripples of delight through her.

"I'm sorry," he gasped. "I'll do...better. Next time."

She giggled. She couldn't help it. He sounded so
winded when she was still soaring with giddy delight.
His hand was clumsy as he tried to touch her face.

He clearly had little strength left, but he stroked her cheek.

"I got carried away."

She pressed a kiss to his lips. "It was wonderful," she said in absolute honesty. Sure the orgasm had been sweet. Not as explosive as usual, but delightful nonetheless. But her mind was still caught on his look, his expression of...

Her mind stuttered on the word she almost inserted there. *Love* was too loaded a word to be thinking right then. Besides, men were always in love when they were buried hilt-deep in a woman. But it had been kind of like that. He had looked at her in a way that appeared to be love.

"I wouldn't change a second of it," she said. "Really," she added when it looked like he didn't believe her.

He straightened slowly, taking a deep breath as strength returned to his body. "Doesn't matter," he said as he looked at her. "We've got all night and an entire lab worth of toys. It's going to get better."

She arched a brow. "Is that a fact?"

He nodded. "We're locked in. And in case you hadn't realized it..." He gestured to the entire lab. "This is what I do best."

She looked at him, rolled her gaze over the lab and then gave him her best yawn of total boredom. It was a lie, of course. She was beyond intrigued by the possibilities ahead. "I think," she drawled, as she leaned back on her elbows. "You're just going to have to prove it to me."

He opened his mouth to say something. They were still locked together, so she knew he was already rising to the challenge. But at that moment, Claire's too-chipper voice sounded through the room.

"Excuse me, sir."

"Yes, Claire?"

"Sorry to interrupt, but dinner has been served. It awaits your gastronomic pleasure in the conference room."

"Thank you, Claire."

"You're welcome, sir. And Mr. Martell asked me to inform you that you've paid for an excellent bottle of wine."

"Thank you, Claire."

"You're welcome. Bon appétit!"

The lab went silent again. Even the DVD had finished. Which left Sam and her, still locked together.

"Well," he said as he slowly withdrew from her. "We better go eat."

"Good idea," she returned.

And then they both said at the exact same moment, "You're going to need all your strength."

14

"MR. FINN HAS QUITE the bizarre brain, doesn't he?"

Sam pursed his lips and did his best to keep his voice level. "Oh? What do you mean?"

"I'm not criticizing. I'm actually pretty impressed," Julie said as she waved her glass of wine at the lab at large. It was quite a measure of his desperation to have her that he allowed such a thing. Normally, liquids were strictly forbidden in here. And truthfully, the more wine she drank, the more he winced whenever she moved. What if some of it spilled? But she was careful. In fact, she must have seen him wince because she burst out laughing.

"You're terrified I'm going to spill this, aren't you?"

He shrugged. "Um, there's some really expensive, really delicate equipment in here."

"I know. I was being careful, but you're right." She drained her glass. "I just didn't want this excellent vintage to go to waste."

Neither did he. Especially since Roger had stuck him with a $350 bottle of wine. He'd nearly gagged when he'd seen the bill, but Julie was worth it. Even if he, personally, would have preferred a cheeseburger and soda to the oysters, artichoke hearts and high-priced merlot.

They'd had quite the laugh together at the array of aphrodisiac foods, but Julie had entered into the adventure with her customary relish. And that made everything all the more fun for him. At her urging, he ate foods that would never have crossed his lips before. He did *not* want to know what was in the goat soup labeled "Mannish Water." And at his urging, she drank the exorbitantly expensive wine. And now they were wandering through the lab while he tried to explain what everything was.

He leaned back against his case of failed circuit board designs. "Um, you were saying about Finn's bizarre brain?"

"He's just so scattered. I suppose that's an inventor's brain for you. A little of this. A little of that. Robotic strawberry picker over there—"

"Yeah, that isn't even remotely practical."

"Solar-powered vacuum cleaner there—"

"Not one of the better ideas."

"Nah, it's great if you store your cleaning products in a sunroom."

"Or need to vacuum your lawn." Then he leaned back against a table. "That had been the idea, actually. Solar-powered leaf—"

"Yeah, yeah," she interrupted. "I get where he was going. Green products are a good idea. As is the strawberry picker, too. It's just scattered, you know. The bizarre meanderings of a genius mind."

"Or a bored one," he said as he wandered through his own lab. "That device there began after watching a news story on a girl who had died from an insect bite while picking strawberries. This one here, from a PBS special on third-world sanitation."

"And the lawn vacuum?"

"I didn't want to rake leaves."

She hooked a lab stool with her foot and hauled it close. "You? That was your idea?"

Oops. Caught. "Well, Finn lets me tinker here, too."

"And what do you think of Mr. Finn's prodigiously scattered brain?"

Sam fiddled with a small soldering rod for circuit boards, unplugged it and put it in its appropriate place on the shelf. He'd have it down tomorrow for something or another, but for the moment, it was put away.

"Come on," Julie urged as she spun a circle on the lab stool. "Give me the dirt. What do you think about Mr. Finn?"

"I think," Sam said slowly, "that he's hired a ton of engineers to take his fiddling to marketable products."

"Well, yeah, but doesn't it feel a bit like dabbling to you? A little of this, a little of that, but someone else does the hard work? Does he ever see a product through to the end?"

"Of course he does!" he shot back, but in his mind he wondered. Sure, he had at the beginning of RFE. He didn't have an army of employees to handle the grunt work then. But now, he often passed off the follow-through work to subordinates. "I, er, he supervises them closely."

Julie stopped spinning to face him. "Look, I'm hardly one to criticize. He's got the successful, multimillion dollar robotics firm, not me. Obviously it works for him. But, well, I can see why you two are such good friends."

He turned to look directly at her. There was an underlying message there. Something about him/Finn that he suspected he really needed to know. "Okay," he drawled. "You're going to have to explain that."

She sighed and plopped her elbows down on the lab table, nearly upending a toy car motor he'd been fiddling with after watching a Christmas special.

"Look, I've never even met the man, so what do I know?"

He settled onto a stool right across from her, then dropped his elbows down as well, mimicking her pose. "Sounds like you were talking more about me than Finn, so spill it."

She grimaced. "You walk around this lab like you own it. You know every part, every bolt, every circuit board, which means you've spent a lot of time here."

No denying that. "So?"

"So, that means you can go nose to nose with a genius like Finn."

He nodded again because he was Finn. "Yeah, so?"

"So what are you doing with your life, Sam? Quit playing around with toys, with half-assed products and gizmos. Find a passion and run with it."

"Hey," he snapped, straightening his shoulders as he pointed to his favorite projects. "A lot of these have excellent potential!"

"And my guess is that Mr. Finn has offered to build any product you develop, probably with an excellent licensing or royalty fee, yadda yadda."

He waved that away. "Yes, yes. So what are you getting at?"

She sighed, and pushed to her feet as she began to wander through the tables. He followed a few steps behind seeing for the first time how much of a maze he had created here. Damn, it was like negotiating a labyrinth!

"I see this in a lot of creative people, Sam," she said as she idly touched the optic core of a robotic eye. "No focus, no discipline."

"Inventing takes inspiration. Wandering. *Dabbling*."

She nodded. "I know. But it also takes dedication and a clear vision." She gestured to the lab at large. "I don't know what Mr. Finn is doing, but I look at you and I wonder where you're going to be in five years. Ten."

Hopefully still CEO of a multimillion dollar company and still *dabbling* in his lab. And maybe still playing sex games with Julie. He winced. Now that he thought about it, that didn't sound so much a plan as more of the same thing.

"That's what I've been struggling with in my presentation to Finn," Julie continued. "There's no clear market focus which means no clear way to develop a coherent company campaign. And that's because there's no clear *product* focus. It's because Finn lives like this. Tinkering with stuff and hoping he'll develop something great."

"Well," Sam hedged, "it's worked so far."

"Yeah, and maybe that works for him. But what about you, Sam?" she pressed, turning around to look at him. "I'm a goal-setter. I have things to do and places to be all the time. And when I fail at those goals, it hurts. It hurts big-time."

Her eyes went hazy for a moment, and he touched her shoulder in a silent offer of support. She squeezed his hand and gave him a warm smile.

"Sometimes," she said softly, "sometimes I think I'm going to break from the pressure of trying to do everything I planned." She stretched up on her toes and pressed a kiss to his lips. Then before he could deepen the caress, she dropped back onto her heels. "But it's way better than not setting any goals at all. Than..." She waved the lab. "Wandering aimlessly through life."

"I'm not wandering," he said firmly, though again, he wondered. "And all that goal setting means you can miss the best things."

"Like elevator games with a hot maintenance man?" she countered with a grin.

"Yeah," he said as he caught her around the waist and pulled her backward against him. No way could she miss that he was already hard for her.

She closed her eyes in appreciation. "Mmm," she murmured as she wrapped her arms over his. "You're right, of course. You have been the best surprise in all my focused, goal-setting life."

"But?" he asked as he slowly turned her around. "I can hear a but in there."

"But there has to be a happy medium, Sam. Purpose and innovation. I tend to be too driven. Whereas you..."

He sighed and looked in her eyes rather than at the chaos of his own lab. "Whereas I'm stuck in nowhere land just tinkering?"

"Aren't you?" she challenged.

"Yes," he finally confessed, "but not why you think."

"Oh?"

He nodded, carefully setting her aside so that he could gather his thoughts. Having her pressed against his groin was not helping him, so he stepped away from her to pace. "Engineering, building, robotics. All of that is easy for me. Has been since I was a kid."

He stopped talking and turned back to her. She didn't say anything, just stood there patiently listening. It was one of the things he most adored about her. She listened to him when he talked. Not because he was her boss, but because she wanted to understand what he was trying to communicate.

"But these are just things. Toys." He picked up the chassis of a robotic car that was supposed to convert to a helicopter. Flying wheels, he'd called it. It worked in the small toy stage—though incredibly expensive—but not in the large format. He'd envisioned a radio-controlled tray that could be used to carry equipment to handicapped people.

"I tinker, Julie, because I haven't got anything else to do." He looked at her. "Anyone else to do it with."

She smiled, her expression going soft. But her words came out a bit more harsh. "Nice try, Romeo, but I don't buy it."

He straightened, insulted. That had *not* been an elaborate come-on. "I meant every word!"

"I'm sure you did, Sam," she said. "But if you want to fill your life with people, get out of the lab! Go bowling! Meet people!"

He sighed. "It's not that easy."

"It isn't easy for anyone. But you're sexy, smart and—"

"And lazy," he abruptly realized. "I have everything I want here. Why look for more?" He moved off the table to come back to her side. "God, I didn't even realize what I was missing until I met you."

She walked easily into his arms. "And now?" she pressed. "Now what are you going to do?"

He arched his brows. "Other than watch you orgasm until you scream?"

She rolled her eyes with mock boredom. "Been there, done that. What have you got for me that's new?"

"Sex toys?"

"Hmm. Anything else?"

He nodded. "I promise to think about what you've said, Julie. Really think about it. Maybe it's time for me to work on something until the very end again."

"Or maybe rearrange how you look at things," she offered. "You've been playing with toys, putting things together and seeing if it's marketable, right?"

He nodded. That's exactly what he was doing.

"How about going the other way? Get out, meet people, see a need and find a way to fill it robotically. Then you'll put together a product that Mr. Finn can really use."

He looked at her, his heart swelling. Damn, she was good for him, made him look at everything in his life in a whole new way.

"And what about you?" he challenged as he began to nuzzle her neck. "What are you going to promise me in return for a half dozen screaming orgasms?"

"The drink or the experience?"

He nipped at her shoulder. "What do you think?"

"I think," she said as she pulled back enough to look seriously into his eyes, "that I promise to rethink my plans about not bringing you into the equation."

He stilled, his whole body startled by a surge of desperate hope. Was she promising to stay in Chicago? To have a real relationship with him? Not just a three-week fling?

"No promises," she said as she pressed a finger to his lips. "But I swear I'll think about it. About you." She arched a brow at him. "That is what you want, right? For me to...for us—"

"Yes," he said against her finger. "Yes, that's what I want." Then he abruptly coiled his tongue around her finger and sucked it into his mouth. She gasped and pulled away, but her eyes had darkened with hunger.

"Well, then, Elevator Man. What you got planned for me tonight?"

He reached behind her and picked up a length of cording. "Did you know that there's more up here than just the lab?"

"No," she said as she twisted, trying to see what he had behind her back.

"Well, there is." He quickly looped the cord around her wrists. "And I think it's time you saw it all."

15

JULIE TRIED TO MOVE her hands forward, but they were tied tight behind her back. Not painful, just secure. She hadn't a clue how he'd managed to do that while hugging her in front, but dang, he'd been quick with the restraints.

A shiver of unease traveled down her spine, but it was matched by a thrill of excitement. Still, she had to know. "Um, you seem very capable with those restraints. Have you done this before?"

He laughed. "Not like you think. Not with a person. But believe me when I say that I have handled things with wheels and other moving parts most of my life. You get quick with your hands when there are moving gears around."

Made sense. Okay, so he wasn't a closet dom. That made the unease disappear and the excitement build. "So what exactly are you planning here?"

She was standing in the middle of a lab, her hands tied behind her back. Hardly the scene for a seduction. But with Sam, she never knew what to expect. That was half the fun.

"Well," he drawled as he stood back and looked at her. "Have you ever been tied up?"

She shook her head, her thoughts whirling. "Tied up," she murmured, as if toying with the idea. Truthfully, she was already fully on board. She leaned forward, already loving that she felt so safe with him. Which left her free to really explore the boundaries. "My, how you tease. But we both know that I'm the one in charge, restraints or not."

She expected the macho man in him to bristle, but he didn't. In fact, he grew even more relaxed, and his eyes sparkled with challenge. "Is that so?" he asked.

"Of course it is," she said with an airy tone. "Make me go down on you, make me lick you, suck you, stroke you. At the end of that, who's the one going to be begging me to finish him?"

As she expected, his jeans grew tighter at her words. His eyes darkened and his nostrils flared. Yes, she loved a man who liked to hear her talk dirty. But beyond those reactions, he didn't move an inch. Instead, he reached over to the computer on Mr. Finn's desk and tapped a few keys. What was he doing? She listened closely for the sounds of what was changing in the lab, but didn't hear a thing. Meanwhile, he straightened away from the keyboard to smile at her.

"Well, as delightful as that sounds, it's not what I have in mind for you. Maybe tomorrow."

"Really?" she said. "Do tell."

He shook his head. "All in good time." Then he touched her shoulder, guiding her around a floor-to-ceiling bookcase of manuals. "This way, please."

She hesitated, her gaze going to the opposite direction. Back to the main entrance to the lab. "Um, what if Mr. Finn comes back? I mean, shouldn't we take this somewhere else?"

"Um, no," he said slowly. "I, uh, I texted him during dinner. Asked if I could work in the lab alone tonight."

She frowned. "He lets you do that?"

"Sure. Especially when he's on the town clubbing."

She straightened. "That doesn't sound like the reclusive Mr. Finn."

"Well," Sam hedged. "Truthfully? He likes to pretend that he's a hot guy out on the town. Likes it if we try and keep up that image for him."

She shook her head. "Doesn't sound like the press I read on him."

Sam laughed. "I didn't say he was good at keeping up that image. In reality, he's got a house up near Northwestern University. Calls up some of his professor friends and they game all night long."

Now that sounded like something a true geek would do. "What kind of games?"

"Warcraft, classic D&D, he's got a whole slew of things he and his buddies play."

"Huh," she said, filing the information away. After all, it never hurt to learn more about her potential employer.

"Which means, *slave,* that I have all night to do as I will. With you."

She smiled, trying to decide what part she would play tonight. They'd already done the submissive secretary bit. Tonight, she'd go for defiant, powerful, strong despite her weakened position. With that in mind, she tossed her hair back from her face.

"Do as you will, master," she drawled. "But I'm still going to be the one in control."

"Really? How's that?"

She shrugged. "No matter what you do to me, you're going to be hard. For me. You're going to desire me. You're going to want to ram yourself thick and hot and hard…into me."

"And that's winning for you?"

"Having you sweating, straining, hungry for me? Thinking of nothing but being in me? Oh, yeah," she drawled. "That's winning."

"Deal," he said.

She frowned. What had she just done? Had he out-maneuvered her somehow? "Uh, come again?"

"No, sweet Julie. You're going to come again and again and again. And I'm going to just sit back and watch because I think that is the sexiest thing ever. Watching you fly apart."

Woah. Everything in her went wet at his words. She cleared her throat. "And how does that make you the winner?"

"Because you're going to beg me, sweet Julie. The moment you plead for me, well then, at that moment—"

"You will be in control," she finished for him. My, she did love the way the man thought. "I understand the terms, master," she answered primly. "And I accept the challenge."

"Well then, slave. This way."

She went willingly. Hell, yes, she went willingly. This was turning into the best Friday night ever! She added a little extra lilt to her hips as she moved, though it was awkward given that her hands were still tied behind her back. They moved around the bookcase and back into a short dark passageway.

"What is this?"

"Finn's living quarters. He's got that house in Evanston, but really, he lives here."

She peered down the hall to what was obviously his bedroom. She couldn't see much, just the shadowy outline of a huge bed and a ton of books on the floor. But Sam wasn't leading her there. Instead, he opened another door to a large…playroom?

The room was big, easily as large as the conference room. The very center of the room had low chairs scattered about the floor. Soft, velvety black, they were lightweight and yet allowed someone to recline and game at ease. The largest chair was facing the far wall which was dominated by a huge screen and speakers. She saw a small table below it that had a Wii and a few remotes. Right now, the screen was displaying a medieval sex/torture room complete with wall sconces, naked writhing women and ripped, Adonis-like men carrying devices that looked like medieval vibrators.

"Wow," she said, truly impressed. "Someone's been playing on the internet."

He snorted. "It took me about thirty seconds to find this online."

She arched her brow at him. "What will Mr. Finn think of what you downloaded onto his screen?"

Sam smiled. "Are you kidding? This was his idea."

She stilled, turning back to him. "You didn't tell him about us, did you? I mean, that would be creepy. You know, sitting across the conference table with him, pitching a story idea, and knowing that he knew that we—"

"It's private, Julie. Just between us. I swear."

"But if it was his idea—"

"To download images to display on screen." He reached over and picked up a remote. "There's a ton of them." At the touch of a button, he scrolled through a beautiful beach scene, complete with naked girls playing volleyball. Then an island sacrifice of a virgin at the volcano. Then snow bunnies—the human female variety—coming in off the slopes with a come-hither grin. There were more, all of them sexual, all of them rather interesting.

"Quite the horndog, isn't he?" she drawled.

"Only lately," he answered as he flipped back to the original sex/torture chamber. "He has normal views as well, famous artwork, serene sunsets, that kind of thing."

"How very prosaic," she drawled, as her gaze went back to Sam. He was looking at a particular writhing woman on the screen. She was stretched out, spread eagle on the rack.

"See something you like?" she drawled.

"Hmm?" he responded, turning back to her. "No, I was just thinking that she isn't tied right, given how much she's moving."

She looked back at the screen, nodding as she realized he had a point. Trust Sam to be aware of all the details.

"Your restraints will be more thorough," he said with a grin.

Her gaze cut back to his with a start of surprise, and he gestured to the wall behind her. She turned. This end was obviously the workout area. A stationary bike and a treadmill occupied a corner beside a rack of free weights, and some huge strength training apparatus. It looked like a big rectangular arch made of steel. Pulleys and cables ran along all the sides and jutting from all four corners were clips with various attachments.

Sam walked over to one and picked up a thick leather bracelet that buckled on.

"Are you ready, slave?" he asked as he opened the bracelet. She saw immediately that it was lined on the inside so it wouldn't abrade or hurt.

She flashed him a wicked grin. "Are you?"

"Oh, yeah." He leaned behind her and undid the cord binding her wrists. Her arms fell forward and she breathed a sigh of relief. The restraints hadn't been painful, but it was nice to let her blood flow freely again.

"Okay?" he asked.

She nodded as she rolled her shoulders. "Peachy!"

"Good. Strip naked, slave."

She flashed him a coy grin. "You don't want to help me?"

"Nope," he drawled, as he walked back to the largest chair. He spun it around, then settled down into it, letting it rock backward as he put his hands over his head. "I like to watch."

She laughed at his movie reference, then proceeded with her orders. She was, after all, his slave for tonight. But just because she had to strip didn't mean she had to make it easy on him. She gestured to the screen behind him. "Got a stripper app?"

He frowned and pulled out the remote. It took a few moments of button pushing, but pretty soon the whole back wall was lit up with a woman pole dancing. "That work?" he asked.

"We'll see," she answered. And then she began.

She'd never thought of herself as particularly sexy. Not unsexy, but not stripper porn sexy. After all, her breasts were average size, not double-Ds, and her legs were long, but not model long. But it didn't matter. With Sam sitting there, his gaze hot on her body, she felt

Marilyn Monroe sexy. And with the screen behind him showing her exactly what to do, she had no problem getting into the striptease.

She began slowly with hip circles and the slow unbuttoning of her trousers. She'd barely gotten the zipper down, though, when Sam held up his hand.

"One second. I need a better view." He scooted his chair forward to right in front of her. "This way, I can touch, too," he said.

The idea had her nipples tightening almost painfully. "Ready to call it quits and just do me?" she taunted.

"Are you begging for me?"

"Not hardly."

"Then you better start stripping, slave."

She gave him an arch look. "Prepare to drool, master."

She began working it as best she could. She wasn't particularly flexible, she wasn't particularly athletic anymore either. But she was coordinated enough to mimic the pole dance on the screen, using the steel poles of the cabled monstrosity behind her. And when a move went beyond her comfort zone, she adapted it or, a couple times, went for it anyway.

Despite his teasing statement, Sam did not touch her once, though she saw his hand twitch. In fact, she even strutted close to him hoping he would haul her down to the floor. But he didn't. He just watched, his breath getting deeper, his groin getting harder, and his mouth did indeed go slack in stunned surprise every now and then.

Well, she thought with a healthy dose of satisfaction, *who knew I had an inner stripper?* And damn if it wasn't getting her hot and bothered, as well. She was down to her thong and heels when he held up his hand. His voice was thick with lust, but she heard him nonetheless.

"Stop, slave!"

She was on all fours, stalking toward him like a stage cat. She'd intended to take things into her own hands, so to speak, and start giving him a lap dance. Or a hand job. Or anything that would push him over the edge. But clearly, he was wise to her. With a flick of his wrist, he turned off the stage show on the screen behind his back. The sex/torture chamber reappeared.

"Take it all off now, slave," he said, obviously trying for a bored tone of voice. It didn't work. She knew he was rock-hard. But she obviously hadn't pushed him to the point where he was begging her to straddle him.

It was harder to strip out of her thong without the erotic music. But she managed to peel the wet thing off while trying to entice him over her shoulder. She hadn't realized how much dancing sexy would turn her on; oh yeah, she wanted him bad.

Keeping with her power persona, she snapped her thong at him and then faced him, legs spread, hands on her hips. All she wore were her black heeled pumps with the flirty bow in the back. Let him try to resist her now.

"Heels, too," he said, though his hands were gripping her thong like a lifeline.

"Are you sure?" she challenged as she stalked closer to him.

He abruptly snapped her thong right back at her. "Yes, I am, slave. Now take them off or admit that you have lost this game."

"Never!" she shot back. Then she kicked off her heels. She didn't need stilettos to be strong, anyway. Once again, she faced him, legs spread, hands on hips.

He looked at her and licked his lips. It wasn't an intentional movement, but a reaction, she was sure. She was getting to him big-time.

"Back up between the poles," he ordered.

She turned around and strutted into position. She put all her attitude into really making all the right things jiggle. He growled, low in his throat and she nearly crowed her victory. But then she felt his breath hot along her back. His hands gripped her hips, large and possessive as they held her tight. She wanted to lean back into him. She tried pushing her butt backward. Lord, she would have loved him to fill her right then, right there. But he didn't let her lower body move. She arched backward, thrusting her breasts upward to give him a perfect view and hoped that he would need to touch them, kiss them, anything!

No luck. He held her firm even as her shoulders hit the hard wall of his chest. Then he spoke, his breath caressing her ear, his very presence seeming to dominate the air she breathed.

"Turn around slowly, slave," he said. "Then present your arms and legs for shackles."

Shackles? Oh, right. The leather cuffs. She did as he bid, though she tried to stroke and touch him while she moved.

"Wider," he ordered.

She spread her legs.

"Now hold your arms out from your sides."

She did that as well. He stepped back and looked at her, a dark gleam in his eyes.

"Perfect. Don't move."

It was harder than expected. The way he looked at her was so thrilling. He watched her with a hunger like a wolf starving for his next meal. Or maybe for his mate.

Either way, she felt his interest, felt every tingling caress from his gaze across her skin. Her nipples tightened to hard points, her belly quivered in anticipation and her breath came in short pants of desire.

How could he turn her on so much with just one look? She licked her lips and his gaze zeroed in. Then, because she knew he was watching, she slowly drew her lower lip inside, biting it slightly. When his nostrils flared, she pursed her lips and gave him a soft kiss.

"Do you want me, Sam? Right now?"

"Are you begging me?"

She grinned. "Nope. You?"

He shook his head. "I haven't even started what I planned for you tonight."

He hadn't? The idea was really titillating. "Well, what are you waiting for, *master?*" she taunted. "I'm getting cold." It was a lie. She was hotter than a bonfire.

Without taking his eyes off of her, he clicked a couple more buttons on the remote which he'd clipped to his jeans. "I've bumped the thermostat another degree. Tell me if you're really cold. But my guess, this isn't from the cold." He abruptly tweaked one of her nipples and she gasped in reaction, her belly contracting in one long ripple of delight.

"Don't move," he ordered again, then he bent to work. He put cuffs on her ankles and wrists and attached weights to the cables. Everything was at rest, so long as she didn't move. But the minute she tried to close her legs or arms, the weights provided resistance. She could move them if she wanted to, if she needed to. But it would take effort.

"Can you undo your cuff if you needed to?" he asked.

She experimented. She could bend down and undo

her ankles, though she was straining her abdominals to do it. As for her wrists...

"Nope."

He made the weights lighter, and she silently swore to work out more. A girl needed to be in shape to be a sex slave!

"How about now?"

She tested it. She could reach both cuffs now with some strain, but she pretended to be too weak. "A little lighter," she said.

He frowned at her, but complied. Not enough for her to fling the weight around, but lighter than he probably wanted.

"And there's one last thing."

She arched a brow at him. It was all she could do, standing there buck naked and tied at her wrists and ankles.

"Just give me a moment." He walked over to the door and pulled it open. In rolled another mechanical spider-like thing. Only this one rolled on three wheels, while six other arms extended upward with various attachments. Two held a tray of interesting devices, including the vibrator in the video.

"That cannot be a real product," she said, looking at the thing.

Sam picked it up. "I have no idea. I just saw it on the video and made one up. It's not hard."

Obviously not for him! She wouldn't have a clue how to start constructing a vibrating toy.

"Though when I get more time, I'd like to refine the hot and cold settings."

She blinked. The dildo had temperature settings?

He flashed her a wicked grin, then began adjusting the height of the various mechanical arms in relation to her. He thumbed his remote and two robotic arms wrapped around her waist with cold precision. There was nothing erotic at all in the placement except when he winked at her.

"That's to keep you from falling over while you're writhing. I didn't have time to fit it for padding but the metal won't abrade your skin."

"I'm seeing a lot of talk here," she said with false bravado. "Trust me when I say, I have no inclination to writhe at the moment."

"Hmm," he said as he slid his free hand between her thighs. He went slowly, flowing his fingers over every part of her. He found her moisture easily—there was enough of it—and slowly, torturously, slid it around.

She was squirming within seconds, her breath coming out in stuttered pants. And then she felt it. The vibrator, slipping easily inside her. She gripped it with her internal muscles. How could she not? It was right there, and even though it wasn't Sam, it still felt good.

"And now the pièce de résistance!" he said. She blinked at him.

"I'm going to hold this," he explained, as he showed her a long stick fitted with feathers, of all things. "And you're never going to know where or when or how it's going to touch you because you're going to be wearing this."

A blindfold. He walked around behind her and carefully covered her eyes. Within seconds, she couldn't see a thing.

"There we go," he quipped with a low laugh. "I think it's time to begin."

16

JULIE FELT LIKE SHE WAS wrapped up like a Christmas turkey except that she was spread eagle, naked and…and…oh, wow! Sam had started suckling the nipple on her one breast.

She ducked her head to see, but of course she was blindfolded so that didn't help her at all. Instead, the darkness gave her nothing else to focus on except each sensation as it flowed through her body. He'd started on the other breast. A gentle pinching then slow rotation of his tongue. Clockwise. Counterclockwise. Then it stopped.

"Sam!" she cried. "This is…this is…" Taking too long!

"Are you crying uncle?" he asked from right behind her.

She jumped and the machine naturally went with her. And when she moved, it felt almost unbearable. But she wasn't going to admit that yet. "Of course not," she answered clearly.

"Then I think you meant to say 'master!'"

Oh, right. "Okay, master. This is getting…" Her mind

fuzzed out. He was stroking her body with his fingers. No place erotic. Just her neck, her belly, her lower back. Random brushes, but she liked it. A lot. *He* was touching her and—

"Oh!" Abruptly the dildo inside her got cold. Not ice-cold, but wickedly uncomfortable. Which was weird because it was vibrating, too, which was a nice feeling. A low, deep vibration that seemed to rumble up her spine. Nice. But coupled with the cold was just bizarre.

She felt his lips across her belly, murmuring. "Don't you mean, 'Oh, master'?"

"Just oh," she said.

"You're gorgeous, you know," he said, this time against her right hip. His hand spread wide across her belly, warming her skin but also stroking her with a kind of worship. He liked to touch her, she could tell. No one spent so much time brushing, stroking and caressing unless he enjoyed it.

"Come for me, Julie," he said against her back. His breath was hot, right at the base of her neck and she shivered in delight. He kissed her there. Then she felt the point of his tongue stroke tiny circles that made her shiver.

"Some commands are difficult to obey, master," she gasped. She was hot, all right. But she wasn't at the orgasmic edge quite yet.

"Then let me help you."

His hands circled her. He was standing behind her, but she felt him move around. She felt his hands brush around her breasts, and then—most exquisite—his lips on hers. She tried to kiss him back. She tried to deepen their connection, but he pulled away too soon.

"Come for me, Julie," he said again.

"Sam…" she began, but her word was cut off by a gasp. The dildo inside her had begun to warm. It didn't feel alive, exactly, but it was heat that radiated through her belly. After the cold from earlier, this felt doubly wonderful. The nipple action had started again, too. Steady suction, gentle twisting. All on its own, it wasn't enough to do more than get her excited. But added to the dildo, she was building fast.

"Touch me, master." She almost said "Sam." She wanted his hands on her body, but had to remember the game. "Touch me like you want to."

"Okay," he answered. And then Sam began working the vibrator between her thighs.

Oh, lord, he was stroking her clit with it. Up and down, he stroked her. Her pleasure built like a tornado, swirling through her belly and expanding through her body.

"Oh! Oh!" She was panting, her body experiencing everything at once. It was almost too much to understand, so she stopped trying. She just felt everything at once. Soon… soon…

A tiny zap of electricity shot through her clit straight into her brain. Like a lightning bolt throughout her entire body. She burst into pleasure, every cell exploding with the power of that one tiny jolt.

She screamed. She writhed. And when the sensations became too much, she started gasping. "Stop! Stop!"

Everything mechanical stopped, but her body continued to roll in waves of pleasure.

"Oh, yes!" he cried. Sam's voice. Sam's joy. At her orgasm. "God, you're incredible like that," he said.

He was holding her. She didn't know when he'd crossed to support her back, but he was there. She was cradled in his arms, and just like that another bolt of lightning struck. This one wasn't physical. It came as a revelation, but the impact was no less shocking.

She loved him. She loved that he was gentle even as he pushed her to explore places she'd never imagined she'd go. She loved that he enjoyed *her* pleasure. She also loved that he supported her dreams, was nice to kids, and that she felt stronger, safer and just downright awesome when she was with him. Added to that was his intelligence, his quiet strength and the way they could talk seriously or sit in silence without any hint of awkwardness, and that made Sam one hugely potent package.

And she loved him. Completely. Awesomely. She loved him.

Suddenly, she had no wish to play with his toys. She wanted him. She wanted Sam the man and nothing else.

With an impatient grunt, she forced her arms together and pulled off the blindfold. She'd faked how hard it was to manipulate her arms, so it was an easy step next to unbuckle her cuffs. Each wrist restraint released and the weights dropped to the stack with a loud clang.

"Julie?" Sam said, his body tensing. "Julie!"

"Get them off me," she said, not because she was repulsed, but because she needed him.

He scrambled to obey, obviously worried that she hadn't enjoyed her descent into mechanical sex-games, and she didn't have the breath yet to explain. Or maybe it was the courage she lacked.

She loved him. But it was so complicated. She was going back to Nebraska in two weeks! He had a job here, and there was no way he could have access to this kind of lab in Nebraska even if he wanted to follow her.

All these thoughts ran through her brain in a second, her mind flashing on possible futures in a whole gamut of directions.

They all began with her telling her revelation to Sam, then spiraled out from there. He could laugh, and it would be torture. He could love her back, which would be amazing until he refused to leave Chicago. She would flounder with no support and no job, become a bitch because she always was one when she wasn't working. He would hate her, and they would break up. Then she'd have to move back to Nebraska heartbroken and jobless and anything from weeks to months to years older.

Then there was that other possibility. The yearned-for, hoped-for soul mate. Oh, hell, could she have that with Sam? Could they make a life of it?

She finally had everything off of her so that she could turn to look directly at Sam. His eyes were wide, his expression anxious.

"What happened?" he asked. "Are you all right?"

She nodded mutely. How did she put everything she was thinking into words? It was so new to her. Maybe it was the result of a really amazing orgasm? But it didn't feel like that. If anything, it felt *more* real than mere physical sensation. Better to focus on right now. On what she wanted at this second and not worry about anything else.

"I don't want toys anymore, Sam," she said softly. "I just want you."

They weren't touching anymore. They'd had to separate for him to pull off her ankle cuffs and push his robotic sex-machine out of the way. She moved toward him now, and he gathered her in his arms. But his touch was tentative, his expression still confused.

"Is this part of the game?" he asked. "Julie, are you—"

"I'm fine, and this is no game." She pulled his face to hers. "That thing was, well, it was great. Seriously twisted, but kinda awesome, too. But it's not you, Sam. As wonderful as that was, I want *you*."

He blinked, comprehension slowly filling his expression. "That's all I've ever wanted, Julie. The rest was just—"

"Games. Toys. I know. But not this time. Just be with me."

He looked at her, his expression shifting from shock to desire to humble awe. Her ego might have been stoked by his obvious worship, except that she knew her face showed the same things. She loved him. That was both humbling and absolutely incredible all at once.

"Sam—"

"Uncle," he said softly.

She blinked. "What?"

"Uncle. I give. I—"

She pressed his fingers to his mouth. "Stop talking, Sam. Just take me to bed."

He nodded against her hand. And then, he abruptly scooped her up in his arms. Seconds later, he was striding down the hallway and into the bedroom. He didn't bother with lights. There was enough spilling in from the hallway anyway for her to see. And he, apparently, didn't care to see as much as touch. His hands were all over her the moment he set her on the bed. She was no less impatient, but his clothing was in the way.

"Naked, Sam," she urged. "Get naked."

He sucked in a breath and pulled away from her. Together, they stripped him and then, hallelujah, she was able to caress him. His penis was in her hands before his shirt hit the floor. Finally, she was able to stroke him, to cup him, to suck him as he had been doing to her.

"Oh, God, Julie…" He pulled her off. She didn't want to go, but he insisted. "I'm too close," he rasped. Then he fumbled with his jeans on the floor, pulling out a condom from the pocket.

She looked at him, her thoughts still spinning. She had wanted to suck him until he exploded. When had that ever happened? Yeah, she understood that each partner got their turn, and she enjoyed giving, but this was a whole new level of need. She wanted to pleasure *him,* and didn't really care at all about herself.

Even more shattering, part of her didn't want him to use a condom. What would it be like to have his baby? To spend their lives together raising a family. His children, their life, a happily ever after. Was it even possible? The hope blossomed within her, as potent as her newfound love.

"You're beautiful," she rasped.

"It's too dark in here for you to see much of anything," he returned.

"I see you," she answered. "I see so much." Possibilities. Potential. A future, or a zillion possible futures. "I lo—"

"I can't wait," he said before she got the words out. Then he scooped her hips out from under her, drawing her to the edge of the bed in one swift motion. He leaned forward, placed himself exactly, and slowly, exquisitely, tenderly pushed himself inside.

God, this was so right! She looked into his eyes. She touched his face. She feathered her fingers across his jaw and lips. His expression was so intense, his body so perfect as he began the slow withdrawal before an equally wonderful thrust.

"Yes," she whispered. Meaning yes to everything. Yes to her love. Yes to the risk. Yes to whatever the future held for him and her. Yes.

But she didn't get all the words out. There wasn't time as Sam's body tightened. His thrusts came faster, his power building. He groaned, low and deep in his throat. And then, his eyes glazed over.

He tried to move his hand, he obviously wanted to roll his thumb over her clit, but she grabbed him. After everything earlier, she was already there. Or close enough that it didn't matter. It was almost as though what their bodies were doing was secondary. She was with him. She was opening up to her love for him, no matter what it meant. She loved him, and that was a wondrous thing.

He slammed into her. Once. Twice. Then he shuddered, releasing a stuttered moan. And his pleasure pushed her over as well. Rippled through her. Joy. Wonder.

Love.

JULIE RELUCTANTLY STRUGGLED up from the depths of sleep. She didn't want to wake. She didn't want to move. She felt warm and languid where she was, tucked tight to Sam's side in a massive bed. But she had to get up.

She cracked an eye. "Bathroom?" she croaked.

"Mmmumph," was Sam's response. His face was tucked into her neck, and she felt the vibration more than heard the word. Either way, it wasn't a specific enough answer.

Forcing herself, she shifted away from him. Aw, hell, it was cold without him. "Sam, where's the bathroom?"

He sighed and flopped onto his back. "Bathroom light on," he commanded in a loud voice.

A room off the bedroom suddenly flared too bright. She shielded her eyes, but at least now she knew where to go. Stumbling forward, she made it to the bathroom. She didn't really want to wake up, but some things were inevitable. By the time she'd finished washing her hands, her eyes had adjusted to the glare and her consciousness was fully engaged.

She'd just had a lovely day, an incredibly fabulous night, and could look forward to an amazing weekend. She was in love with Sam, but had yet to tell him. She was already thinking of a dozen possible scenarios for sharing the news when she left the bathroom.

She was trying to figure out how to turn off the light when her gaze snagged on a picture on the dresser. It was a family photo, clearly from several Christmases ago. There was Mom and Dad in matching Christmas-tree sweaters, probably knitted by mom. A younger Sam stood awkwardly beside his father, looking rather gaunt and geeky with his neat haircut and Christmas-ornament sweater.

Beside Mom was another young man, devilishly handsome with a rakish grin and a blank look in his eyes. The blind brother. And in front was Sam's little sister, looking tan and buff and in the prime of her athletic days.

Julie smiled, picking up the picture and angling it toward the light. Nice picture. Nice family. She couldn't wait to meet them all. And she imagined the interesting responses when Sam met her boisterous, rough-and-tumble brothers. Her parents, she already knew, would embrace him happily. It was her brothers he would have to impress, though she was sure he could manage it.

She set down the picture, taking a moment to look about the bedroom. Sam still lay on his back in bed, the black sheet barely covering him from the belly down. He was in that halfway place of the not yet awake. While she watched, his eyes opened to half mast, then drifted back down.

She meant to go back to bed. She wanted nothing more than to climb in beside him and snuggle back to sleep. Or snuggle to something else. But something kept her right where she was. Something tugged at her brain and kept her standing right there.

She glanced back at the photo. Sam had filled out nicely, she thought. He hadn't had much upper body strength in this photo, but obviously he did now. Clearly he used the free weights in the playroom. The stationary bike as well, she thought, as she remembered him in bicycle shorts.

Her gaze slid back to his sleeping form, her thoughts centering not on him, but on the black sheets. Something about... Oh, yes. She remembered him telling her that his bedroom was all cold colors and metal. Even his sheets were black.

She let herself scan the room at large. Sure enough, even the dresser was an uninteresting black metal thing more appropriate to an office than a bedroom. Then there were the books scattered about the floor as well as a pile of clothing in a hamper in the corner. She recognized Sam's coveralls in there as well as the tee he'd worn yesterday.

And that's when it hit. Sam's clothing was here. Sam's bedsheets were here. Sam's family photo was here. In Mr. Finn's bedroom. Except, obviously, it wasn't Mr. Finn's bedroom.

She flashed on the awkward way he'd said Mr. Finn's

bio had been written by marketing. That it wasn't even the name he really went by. She bit her lip. The CEO's full name was James S. Finn. What did the *S* stand for? Had she ever learned Sam's last name?

More and more pieces fell into place. His familiarity with the lab. The way the voice commands responded to him. Even the freaky undercurrents between him and Roger during her meeting.

"Oh, God. Oh, God." It was true, she realized with horror. Sam was James Sam Finn, CEO of RFE.

Oh, God. There was too much to process. What had she said about Mr. Finn yesterday? Why had he lied about who he was? Was this some sort of sick game he played with women? Was Roger in on it? Did *everyone* but her know?

Sam's eyes were now open, his expression rapidly shifting to alarm. "Julie?"

She backed away from him, her body shuddering with a physical revulsion. It had all been a lie! She pointed a shaking finger at the photo on the dresser.

"That's you," she accused. "That's your family there!"

He pushed himself up to a sitting position, his face scrunched as he squinted. "Julie? Hell, Julie, I can't see."

She didn't know how to respond to that. She didn't know how to respond to *anything*.

"You're him. You're James S. *Finn*."

He stilled at that, his face going pale. Then, slowly, he exhaled, his shoulders slumping.

"Yeah," he said. "Yeah, I am."

"You lied," she said. "Oh, God, *everything* has been one big lie."

"No, no it hasn't!" He shot to his feet and stumbled

around the bed toward her. But she backed up. She couldn't have him touching her right now. Hell, she was having trouble not getting distracted by his naked body.

"It has!" she cried. She'd been about to tell him she loved him. "You're Mr. *Finn!*"

"Julie, you wanted it this way. You called me Elevator Man. You wanted a fantasy, not reality."

It was the truth. She knew it was. But not to this level. She hadn't thought the fantasy extended that far. "You lied about your *name*."

"Julie—"

"I never lied. Not once. Not about who I was."

"Neither did I! It's Finn who's the made-up person. I'm just Sam."

"Stop it! Just stop it!"

She couldn't think. She couldn't handle more. She'd just realized she loved him, and now he wasn't even him anymore! Hell, even her thoughts didn't make sense.

"Just hang on a minute, Julie. Just let me—"

"No," she gasped. "No! Just stop right there."

He was trying to close the distance between them, trying to hold her. But she grabbed the photo off his desk and used it to hold him back from her. It wasn't large enough to really be an obstacle, but it was a message nonetheless. And with the near panic in her voice, he thankfully complied. He stood apart from her, the edge of the frame pressed against his chest. His arms were at his side and his expression was one of desperation.

"Julie, just please, can we talk about this?"

"No," she gasped.

"Julie—"

"No!" She took a deep breath. "You listen to me, okay! Just give me a minute."

He was silent. Obviously, he was giving her the minute. But this was too much. And they were naked. She couldn't think like this!

"I'm going to leave now," she said.

"No!" He lunged forward, but she stepped backward.

"It's not forever, Sam," she said firmly. "It's just until I can get a handle on this."

"So let's talk about it."

"No!" she huffed. "I just need to be alone and quiet and…" Not naked. Both physically and emotionally, she needed to be *not* naked.

She watched his hands bunch and his shoulders tighten. He was fighting this, fighting letting her go. "Just let me get my contacts in. I'll order breakfast. We'll—"

"You'll charm me. You'll sweep me into another sexfest."

He winced. "We'll talk. I swear—"

"I know," she said, though truthfully, she didn't feel like she knew anything at all. "But I can't. Not…" She glanced at the clock at the side of his bed. Big red numbers. "God, it's three in the morning."

"So come back to bed. Get some sleep and we'll—"

"I'm going home, Sam. Don't call me. Let me call you."

"Not going to happen, Julie."

She shoved his picture at him sudden and hard enough that he swayed backward. She reached for anger, deliberately misunderstanding him because she couldn't process anything else. "You're going to lock me up? Keep me here as your slave?"

"You know that's not what I meant!"

"Do I?" she asked, her voice breaking. "I don't even know who you are!"

"I'm your Sam. The same guy I was ten minutes ago, ten hours ago, ten days ago."

"But you're also James S. Finn."

He sighed. "You don't know how many times I tried to tell you."

She blinked, her eyes watering. She was emotionally inside out. She couldn't think. She loved him, she knew she did, and yet... "I have to go."

She spun on her heel and dashed out the door. Thankfully it wasn't hard to find her clothes, though they were scattered about the lab and playroom. She dressed as quickly as she could with a squinty-eyed Sam following her the entire way.

He didn't say anything. He tried a couple times, but she cut him off. She couldn't hear anything he said right then. She promised him she would eventually, just not right that second. It was too much. Just...too much.

So she dressed and left. He went down in the elevator with her, tried once more to talk to her, but she refused. Just like on that first night, he watched until she got into her car. In fact, he stood there in her rearview mirror, his expression so devastated that she started sobbing. And once the tears started, she couldn't stop.

She tried to hold them in. She tried to keep it together just until she made it home. The pain cut so deep. Everything she thought she knew, everything she felt about him... Was it true? Was any of it real? How could he have lied to her?

She turned a corner. Almost home. She didn't hear

the truck horn until too late. And then her head was whipped back as the Silverado plowed into her car. Then wham. Airbag. Pain.

Black.

17

SHE CAME TO AS THE PARAMEDICS pulled her out of her
car. They flashed a penlight in her eyes and asked her
questions. She told them her name and the date. Even
named the current president. Then when they asked if
there was someone they could call for her, she just said
no. There was no one she wanted to see, not even Karen,
though Sam's face burned in her thoughts.

"Just let me sleep," she murmured, then she closed
her eyes. They didn't, of course. She had a possible head
injury, so they kept her awake and alert enough to relive every stupid moment of this evening. She came to
no brilliant conclusions except that she was an idiot for
trying to drive and sob her eyes out at the same time.
And now she had medical bills that she couldn't pay on
top of everything else.

Eons later, they finally left her alone in her hospital
bed. Then the painkillers finally, beautifully, kicked in.
But her last thought was of Sam and that the tears felt
hot against her bruised face.

THEY DISCHARGED HER the next day. She called Karen
to drive her home. Her friend was full of questions, of

course, but one look at Julie's battered face and she asked just the one.

"Do you want to talk? Or just forget for the moment?"

Julie couldn't bring herself to smile, but she did manage a grateful look. "Forget," she whispered.

"Agreed. For now," Karen said. Then she got Julie her prescription of painkillers and drove her home.

SAM WAS GOING INSANE! Two days of total silence from Julie. He'd left a zillion messages on her cell, but no call. She hadn't come to work. In fact, Web Wit and Wonder had been dark, so he couldn't even talk to her friend. Every other minute, he thought about going to her home, but she'd told him she needed space. Considering the depth of his lies, a couple of days wasn't too much to ask. Except it was killing him.

He was completely useless at work, alternating between snapping at his employees and hiding in his lab. Except that was no sanctuary because everywhere he looked reminded him of Julie. She'd been in his lab, she'd touched just about every piece of equipment here, and she'd been touched by him here, too. But his bedroom and his playroom were worse, so he stayed here.

He sent flowers, watched the security cameras in front of her suite, did everything but storm her little apartment. He'd just made up his mind to do it anyway when he glanced one more time at the security monitors. Was that her friend Karen? Yes! She was right now walking down the hallway to their suite. He was on his feet in a second, pushing past Roger to get down there pronto.

"Where is she?" he demanded the moment he

crossed the threshold of Web Wit and Wonder. "Where's Julie?"

Apparently, his appearance was rather frightening because Karen spun around with a squeak of alarm. Sam bit his lip, deliberately took a deep breath and tried to moderate his tone.

"Hello, Karen," he said, though the words came out clipped. "Remember me? I'm Sam."

"The elevator man," she returned with a nod.

He sighed. Best to get the truth right out there in the open. "Yeah. I'm also James S. Finn, CEO of RFE upstairs."

Karen's eyes widened in shock, especially as she took in his coveralls and generally disheveled appearance. "Oh," she managed. "That's a surprise."

"Look, I'm going to cut to the chase here. I'm in love with Julie. I need to talk to her, to beg her forgiveness. Where is she?" Had he really just said that out loud? Apparently so because Karen's eyes softened.

"Then those must be from you." She waved to the array of flowers that he'd had delivered. Without someone here to open the office, the bouquets had lined up outside, like a funeral display. He'd sent a bunch to her apartment, too, so there was probably another line there.

"Yeah, they are. So where—"

"She had a car accident."

The words took a moment to penetrate his brain. And when they did, his body responded before he could. His knees went weak, and his heart climbed up into his throat. "Oh. Oh, God. Is she… Was she…" He couldn't even say the words.

"She's fine," Karen answered. "But her cell is dead. Her car, too, for that matter."

"I'll buy her new ones. Is she at her apartment?" He was already spinning out the door before Karen could answer, but he skidded to a stop at Karen's call.

"Wait! She's not there!"

Sam turned back, nearly knocking over a vase of roses in the process. "Where is she?"

Karen bit her lip. "Look, I don't know who you are—"

"I already told you. I'm Sam!"

"Yeah, I know. But I don't really know *you*. Julie said she needed some time to regroup. And to let the bruises fade. She didn't want anyone to bother her."

"I'm not going to bother her!" He was just going to hog-tie her down and *talk* to her.

"Um, forgive me, Sam, but you look exactly like you're going to bother her."

Sam stopped himself from tightening his hands into fists. He stopped himself from doing anything that hinted at the well of frustration he had seething within him. He simply moderated his tone and said in his best CEO voice, "Karen, tell me where she is. I'm just going to talk to her." It was a lie, of course. He knew that the second he was with her, he was going to do way more than just talk. But truly, there would be talking first. There had to be. Then there would be seduction, courting, showering in presents, anything he could think of to keep her in his life.

"Wait a second!" Karen said as she smacked her palm against her forehead. "Duh. You're James Finn, CEO of RFE."

He tried not to grind his teeth. "I just told you that."

"Yeah, I know. But Julie told me to send you an

email. You just took me so by surprise there that I wasn't thinking."

Sam stepped forward, barely restraining his impatience. "What was the message?"

"Um…"

"Damn it! What. Was. The. Message?"

Karen took a step back, her eyes widening in terror. "That, um, she wants a meeting with you."

Every part of his body deflated in relief. She was going to talk to him. She wasn't leaving for Nebraska. "When?" he rasped.

"Tomorrow. Ten a.m."

"Done. But where is she—"

"And there's one more thing…"

He looked at her, trying not to growl when she didn't continue immediately.

"Um, yeah, she wanted me to make it clear that Web Wit and Wonder would *not* be renewing its contract for this office suite. We're closing up."

Sam straightened. "What? No! She doesn't have to—"

"She was firm. And I agreed. We're closing."

Which meant Julie was still going back to Nebraska. Ah, hell.

18

NO AMOUNT OF FOUNDATION could cover a shiner like the one Julie had. The airbag had slammed into the side of her face since she'd been looking at the truck, not straight ahead. It had *not* broken her nose, but had burst what had to be every capillary on the left side of her face. She considered telling everyone she was in training to be a Golden Gloves boxer. Fortunately, no one was looking too closely at her as she pressed the button to call for an elevator.

"Miss Thompson?"

Julie turned around and smiled at the security guard. He wasn't Sam, so she had to immediately squelch the surge of disappointment. It helped that her expression pulled at her bruises. Pain was a great distraction.

"Is there a problem?" she asked.

"Er, not exactly. You're heading up to RFE?"

She nodded. It was time to face Sam, but she was doing it as co-owner of Web Wit and Wonder, not Julie Thompson, recent sex addict. She wore a navy blue, by-the-books business suit, her hair was pulled up in a bun, and there was at least an inch of makeup on her abused face. This was corporate Julie, and she would be the one talking with James S. Finn, CEO. Girlfriend Julie would come later. Maybe.

"Yes, I have a meeting with Mr. Finn at ten."

"I know. He asked that you follow me, please." He gestured down the hallway, away from the elevator bay.

"I'm sorry. What's going on?"

"RFE has its own private elevator. Mr. Finn asked that you use that one."

She tilted her head in surprise. Seriously? Sam had his own private... She immediately put a stop to the ideas racing through her head.

"Very well," she said with forced casualness. "Where is it?"

"In here." He led her through a restricted set of doors to a single huge, rather plain elevator. "It's used mostly for moving equipment," he said as he tapped the button. Then he grinned. "And a few dignitaries."

The doors whooshed open to a bay filled with roses. Dozens of roses in vases set in the corners of the elevator. Julie just stood and stared at them.

"They were outside your suite. A new one every day. Mr. Finn suggested I put them in here so you'd see them before you went upstairs."

She arched her brows at him. So much for her corporate persona. Nothing screamed romance like four-dozen long-stemmed roses. "Well," she said slowly. "Wasn't that thoughtful of him?" Then she stepped into the rose-scented elevator and pressed the button labeled Lab. It was the only other button beyond ground.

She turned and faced front. The guard gave her a quick nod then watched her with an impassive expression until the doors shut. She tightened her grip on her briefcase as the elevator began to lift…then came to a halt midway.

Julie frowned and pressed the Lab button again, though she knew it was useless. This was obviously Sam's doing. She didn't even bother opening the access panel to look for a phone or anything. All she had to do was stand here and wait for his next move. Well, that and control the sudden surge of lust coursing through her veins. After all, their story had begun with "accidental" fondles in an elevator. Who knew what he had in mind now?

She didn't have to wait long. About a minute later, she heard Sam's voice coming distinctly through the elevator ceiling.

"Problem, ma'am?"

She looked up as his face appeared above her. The man was squatting on top of the elevator, looking down at her through an access hatch.

"I appear to be stuck," she said.

"I know the feeling," he said as he carefully maneuvered his toolbox through the opening then dropped it to the floor.

What was that supposed to mean? she wondered. Exactly how stuck could a multimillionaire CEO be?

She didn't get time to ask her question aloud, though, because Sam was busy dropping down in front of her. He moved with a lithe grace, as usual, but he looked a bit haggard. As if the last few days had been unusually tough on him. It was evil of her, but her heart lifted at the sight. She didn't want him to suffer, but it was good to see some indication that their relationship hadn't been just an elaborate game to him.

"Okay," he said. "Let's see..." His voice trailed away as he studied her face.

She flushed, knowing he was staring at her bruises, especially as his mouth tightened into a grim line.

"It looks way worse than it is," she offered.

"Jules..." he said, his voice strangled.

She held up her hand to stop him. "What are we doing here, Sam? Is this another elevator tryst? A return to our glorious sexual past?"

"No!" He shook his head, his expression shifting to desperate. "I just figured it wouldn't hurt to remind you of, um..."

"That the sight of you in a coveralls makes me hot?" she challenged.

He flushed. "Well, yeah."

"Well, okay. So I'm reminded," she said gently. "But sex has never been a problem between us. My issue is with CEO Sam."

He threw out his hands. "This is who I really am, Julie. You gotta know that."

"No, you're not. James Finn is a huge part of you." She grimaced and looked away. "When I think of how I kept at you for not going anywhere with your life. For not pursuing something more than being a janitor—"

"It wasn't bad advice."

"For the CEO of a multimillion dollar company?"

He winced. "For me. For Sam. What you said about me being unfocused is true. Roger has been telling me that for years."

"So why haven't you listened?"

He shrugged. "Because wandering worked. I got to play every day on whatever I wanted, and the money kept coming. Until recently, at least."

She tilted her head, waiting for the rest. "Recently?" she prompted when he didn't continue. "What changed?"

"The economy. The price of my toys." His gaze tightened like a laser onto her face. "You."

She snorted. "Me? I'm just your sexfest date."

He stepped forward and cupped her elbows. She let him. Hell, she wanted to be buried in his arms, but this was too important. That's exactly why she'd worn her ruthless businesswoman attire. So she would be reminded with every breath that she had to think first before she acted.

"You've been more than that from, well hell, from almost the beginning."

She arched her brows at him. She didn't believe that was true. Not for a second.

"It's the truth!" he huffed. "I noticed you because you were a committed, focused businesswoman and yet wore yellow dresses and were this creative dynamo. I saw you in the lobby and I knew even then—on some level—that you were just what I wanted."

She sighed, her heart melting despite her determination to be strong. "Everything we did was built on lies. My fantasies and your lies."

He touched her chin, pulling her gaze back to his. "There's nothing wrong with fantasies, Julie. We're consenting adults. They were fun."

"But that's not enough for a relationship."

"Isn't it? *Wasn't* it a good beginning for what we've built since?"

She pushed away from him, getting to the crux of her problem with their whole situation. "We haven't built anything, Sam! We've played some great games. We've gone on a bowling date."

"Those weren't just little things to me!" he snapped.

"Nor to me," she said softly. But before he could distract her, she held up her hand. "Tell me honestly, as CEO of RFE, is there business for me at your company?"

He bit his lip. "Maybe. You've got good ideas. Roger really was impressed."

"But it'll take time. And it probably won't be anything substantial at first."

He sighed and rubbed a hand over his face. "I warned you, Julie, from the very beginning that it was a long shot. We still may be able to work something out, but—"

"But I'm not interested. Web Wit and Wonder doesn't have that kind of time. As of a few mornings ago, we're officially closing our doors."

He blinked, and she saw all his hopes crash in that one moment. "Julie, we can work something out."

She shook her head. "No, we can't. Not as RFE and Web Wit and Wonder. It's just not going to happen."

He dropped back against the side of the elevator. "Julie…" he whispered, though he clearly had no idea what to say.

"So are we done with our official meeting?" she asked. "Are we done with our pretend game of corporate alliances?"

"It was never pretend," he said, his tone a half growl. "I'm still looking for a way—"

"*Stop looking!*" she cried.

He swallowed. Slowly, she saw acceptance seep into his expression. His shoulders slumped, his gaze dropped to the floor, and he released a sigh that seemed to come from his toes.

"If that's the way you want it," he finally said.

"I do. It's done." Then she took a deep breath. Now was the moment of truth. The real step. "Which means, we can move on to the next relationship. The one between Julie and Sam."

So saying, she dropped her briefcase on the floor and shrugged out of her jacket. Her hands were on the buttons of her blouse when she abruptly froze and looked up at the ceiling.

"Is there a camera in here?"

He shook his head, his eyes widening in surprise. "No cameras."

"Good," she said. "Then it's okay for me to do this." She pulled off her blouse and slipped right out of her skirt. One minute later, she was standing before him in her brand-new black lace thong and bra set, thigh-high hose, and black pumps.

She saw him swallow. She saw him gape. But what she didn't see was understanding flow through his rather impressive brain.

"Remember back in your playroom, way back when I pulled off all the, um, equipment, and I said I wanted you?"

He nodded, but he didn't speak.

"I realized then that I was falling in love with you. That I *am* in love with you." She stepped forward, coming into the circle of his arms. Immediately, he put his hands on her hips and held her with fingers that tightened possessively. "I don't know what I'm going to do now that my company is dead. I've got debts and life decisions ahead—"

"We can work those out, Julie. I swear. I can help you with all of that."

She smiled, stretching closer to him, allowing her naked belly to land against his heavy coverall. "All I know is that I don't want it to end here. I want you in my life while I figure out all the other pieces."

She expected him to say something then. He didn't. Instead, he released a heavy burst of air and dropped his forehead down against hers. And he shuddered, actually shuddered in relief.

"Sam?"

"I love you, Julie. I knew it before, but I hadn't told you who I was. And when I tried, you wouldn't hear—"

"I know," she said. "I had a lot of time to think over the last few days. I remembered all the times you tried to talk to me. I realized that you were trying to get the truth out."

"You're not just an office fling, Julie. You never have been. I need your spark in my life. I need your creativity and your focus, and I need you to drag me out bowling."

"I need you to tell me that I'm strong and that I'll figure things out. Not solve them for me, but be with me while I do it."

"Always, Julie. I love you."

"I love you," she said, at almost the exact same moment. Then she stretched up to kiss him. He met her halfway, and they spent a few wonderful, glorious minutes locked in each others arms.

But then Sam pushed her back. "There's, um, something I need," he said, his voice thick. "Something in my toolbox. Would you mind getting it for me?"

She grinned. "If it's one of these, I think I've got you covered." She reached into her bra and pulled out a condom.

He laughed and pulled it from her hand. "That's great, but that's not what I meant." He gestured behind her at his box. "Would you mind?"

She smiled, flashed him a coy look and turned around. Then making sure she did it slowly and as provocatively as possible, she bent over at her waist, pushed her bottom high and popped open the top of his toolbox. Behind her, she heard him groan in appreciation as his hands curved over her cheeks.

"You're killing me here, Julie."

"That's the point—oh!" She'd finally looked down into the toolbox to see a dark jeweler's box. It was the perfect size for a ring.

She straightened abruptly, turning around to look at him. "No, Sam. It's too soon. It's—"

"Open it."

Her hands were shaking, but she managed to pop it open. Inside it was… She didn't have a freaking clue what it was. "What is this?"

He reached down and gently pulled out what was obviously a ring, but where the stone would be sat a tiny circuit board held by two mechanical hands.

"I knew you'd think it was too soon. But the one thing you don't know about James S. Finn, CEO, is that sometimes things just hit him as perfect. All his best inventions have happened that way."

"I'm not an invention, Sam."

"No, you're not. But our relationship is something we're going to have to work on, to 'invent' together, so to speak." He held the ring up before her, showing her how the hands moved, twisting and shifting the tiny board to keep it level no matter what angle the ring was held at. "I know that I want to marry you. I know that you're the one for me. But until you agree, I want you to wear this prototype."

She laughed, starting to see where he was going. "You're giving me a prototype of an engagement ring?"

"Yes. You tell me when you want to upgrade to a big fat diamond. Just say the word and—"

"Yes! Yes!" she cried as she held out her hand. "I accept your prototype, James Samuel Finn. I will wear it with great pride." And after he slipped it on her finger, she spent more long minutes locked in a very hot kiss. He broke off only when she began stroking the length of him through his coveralls.

"Julie—" he began, but she shrugged.

"If only we could think of something to do while waiting for the elevator to start up again." She gave him an arch look. "I'm ready to start inventing our relationship, Sam. Perhaps you could use a tool or something and help get us on our way."

He was already pulling down the zipper of his coverall. Underneath he had on—oh, my!—nothing at all. "You are by far the best thing that has ever happened to me," he said. "God, I love you."

She helped him out of his coveralls, and she helped herself to a long, sweet caress of his length. She already knew that she wouldn't be wearing Sam's prototype ring for long. She would wait a few months just to be sure. But this man gave her everything she ever wanted in life, and it wasn't money or work or even sex. He just wanted to be with her, to talk to her, to support her and to help her figure things out. He loved her. And she loved absolutely everything about him.

"You know," she drawled as she fitted her body to his. "If this really is your *private* elevator, I've got some suggestions for renovations."

He grinned. "We'll start working on the plans together. This afternoon."

"Yes!" she said as they began to move together. "Oh, God, Sam, yes. To everything!"

Epilogue

A Bachelor Party. Sort Of...

Despite my gravest and most sincere efforts, James Samuel Finn is getting married. I've spent months trying to talk him out of it, but some idiots can't be reasoned with. So, we've got one last chance to talk him out of matrimonial hell, and you're invited.

Please join me—Roger Martell, his best and very ignored friend—in the Presidential Suite of the Chicago Hilton for Sam's bachelor party. Sadly, I may have to miss this glorious event because my doctor has just informed me that the stress of being Sam's CFO is killing me. The doctor thinks I should stop living a high-speed life, and change to a low-stress job.

Fortunately, I have a better idea. I'm going to Chicago's art district to find some new age healer. Let her work her voodoo to bring my blood pressure down. Crystals, aromatherapy, Zen rocks. Whatever. Just so long as it works. Then I won't have to change at all.

So, come along and join the fun!

Date: March 2011
Location: *In Good Hands* by Kathy Lyons

* * * * *

*See below for a sneak peek from our classic
Harlequin® Romance® line.*

Introducing DADDY BY CHRISTMAS by Patricia Thayer.

MIA caught sight of Jarrett when he walked into the open lobby. It was hard not to notice the man. In a charcoal business suit with a crisp white shirt and striped tie covered by a dark trench coat, he looked more Wall Street than small-town Colorado.

Mia couldn't blame him for keeping his distance. He was probably tired of taking care of her.

Besides, why would a man like Jarrett McKane be interested in her? Why would he want to take on a woman expecting a baby? Yet he'd done so many things for her. He'd been there when she'd needed him most. How could she not care about a man like that?

Heart pounding in her ears, she walked up behind him. Jarrett turned to face her. "Did you get enough sleep last night?"

"Yes, thanks to you," she said, wondering if he'd thought about their kiss. Her gaze went to his mouth, then she quickly glanced away. "And thank you for not bringing up my meltdown."

Jarrett couldn't stop looking at Mia. Blue was definitely her color, bringing out the richness of her eyes.

"What meltdown?" he said, trying hard to focus on what she was saying. "You were just exhausted from lack of sleep and worried about your baby."

He couldn't help remembering how, during the night, he'd kept going in to watch her sleep. How strange was that? "I hope you got enough rest."

She nodded. "Plenty. And you're a good neighbor for

coming to my rescue."

He tensed. Neighbor? *What neighbor kisses you like I did?* "That's me, just the full-service landlord," he said, trying to keep the sarcasm out of his voice. He started to leave, but she put her hand on his arm.

"Jarrett, what I meant was you went beyond helping me." Her eyes searched his face. "I've asked far too much of you."

"Did you hear me complain?"

She shook her head. "You should. I feel like I've taken advantage."

"Like I said, I haven't minded."

"And I'm grateful for everything…"

Grasping her hand on his arm, Jarrett leaned forward. The memory of last night's kiss had him aching for another. "I didn't do it for your gratitude, Mia."

Gorgeous tycoon Jarrett McKane has never believed in Christmas—but he can't help being drawn to soon-to-be-mom Mia Saunders! Christmases past were spent alone…and now Jarrett may just have a fairy-tale ending for all his Christmases future!

Available December 2010,
only from Harlequin® Romance®.

HARLEQUIN®

A Romance

FOR EVERY MOOD™

Spotlight on

Classic

Quintessential, modern love stories
that are romance at its finest.

See the next page
to enjoy a sneak peek from
the Harlequin® Romance series.

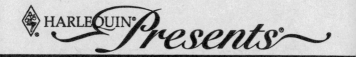

Silhouette® *Desire*

USA TODAY bestselling authors

MAUREEN CHILD

and

SANDRA HYATT

UNDER THE MILLIONAIRE'S MISTLETOE

Just when these leading men thought they had it all figured out, they quickly learn their hearts have made other plans. Two passionate stories about love, longing and the infinite possibilities of kissing under the mistletoe.

Available December wherever you buy books.

Always Powerful, Passionate and Provocative.

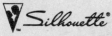

ROMANTIC
SUSPENSE
Sparked by Danger, Fueled by Passion.

RACHEL LEE
A Soldier's Redemption

When the Witness Protection Program fails at keeping Cory Farland out of harm's way, ex-marine Wade Kendrick steps in. As Cory's new bodyguard, Wade has a plan for protecting her—however falling in love was not part of his plan.

Conard County *THE NEXT GENERATION*

Available in December
wherever books are sold.

REQUEST YOUR FREE BOOKS!

2 FREE NOVELS
PLUS 2
FREE GIFTS!

HARLEQUIN®

Blaze™

Red-hot reads!

HB10R

COMING NEXT MONTH

Available November 30, 2010

#579 IT MUST HAVE BEEN THE MISTLETOE...
Kate Hoffmann, Rhonda Nelson, Tawny Weber

#580 PRIVATE PARTS
Private Scandals
Tori Carrington

#581 NORTHERN ESCAPE
Alaskan Heat
Jennifer LaBrecque

#582 UNDER WRAPS
Lose Yourself...
Joanne Rock

#583 A MAN FOR ALL SEASONS
Heather MacAllister

#584 I'LL BE YOURS FOR CHRISTMAS
Samantha Hunter

HBCNM1110